Read All the Best Friends Dog Tales

Stella

Just Gus

Millie

Millie

McCall Hoyle

Illustrations by Kevin Keele

SHADOW
MOUNTAIN
PUBLISHING

Illustrations © 2024 Kevin Keele
Text © 2024 McCall Hoyle

All rights reserved. No part of this book may be reproduced in any form or by any means without permission in writing from the publisher, Shadow Mountain Publishing®, at permissions@shadowmountain.com. The views expressed herein are the responsibility of the author and do not necessarily represent the position of Shadow Mountain Publishing.

Visit us at shadowmountain.com

This is a work of fiction. Characters and events in this book are products of the author's imagination or are represented fictitiously.

Library of Congress Cataloging-in-Publication Data
(CIP data on file)
ISBN 978-1-63993-233-7

Printed in the United States of America   10/2023
Lake Book Manufacturing, LLC, Melrose Park, IL

10 9 8 7 6 5 4 3 2 1

*To my father,
who took me to libraries, bought me all the
books, and taught me to dream big*

In spite of everything, I still believe people are really good at heart.

—ANNE FRANK

Chapter One

I know a lot about humans. I know the pattern of their days—when they rise and when they rest. I even know some of their words, but I do not know my name.

I'm a stray.

I'm good at watching and hiding.

It's what I do.

Watch and hide.

Watch and hide.

Tonight, I hide in the cold shadows behind a row of trash cans. The darkness helps, and so does my grizzled brown-and-black fur. And my small size.

The family across the street doesn't notice me. Their sense of smell is not as good as mine. Plus, they're too busy talking and walking to see me. They glide behind their own dog like they've never thought of hiding from anything ever before—like they enjoy standing unprotected in the bright circles the streetlights cast.

Standing tall, I try to make myself smell bigger and braver than I am. I do not want the older dog to bark and give me away. Thankfully, she barely twitches her nose. She is more interested in getting back to her warm home than alerting her family to my presence. I would like to be warm, too, but first, I need food.

"Is it really going to snow, Daddy?" the young human asks. She trots to keep up with two adults. A ball bobs on top of her hat. I do not like hats. They make human heads look too big for human bodies, and they hide human eyes. They make it hard for dogs to know how humans will behave. But this girl is small and smells like cookies, and her hat has a *ball* on top. So she can't be that bad.

"Oh, it's going to snow." The man looks down at the little girl. His hair shines in the light of the giant moon. "And snow. And snow. They're saying it could be worse than the blizzard that hit Asheville the year I was born."

I shiver as a gust of wind nips at my belly.

The mom pulls the girl toward her, but their puffy jackets hold them apart like a squishy fence. "Thankfully, we have tons of hot cocoa and enough cookie dough to last a lifetime."

"Yay!" The girl runs ahead of them, up the sidewalk to their house.

"You got milk, bread, and batteries, right?" The dad's voice drops as he reaches for the mom's hand.

She takes it and snuggles into his side. "Yep. And eggs. And candles. And pretty much everything else left on the shelves."

He smiles down at her. "I'm good, then—food, family, shelter. That's all I need."

"Yep." She nuzzles her head into his shoulder.

My insides tighten at the sight of them moving together, warm and well fed, like two dogs in a healthy pack. Then the young girl pushes the door to their house open. The old dog wags her tail and trots to catch up. Even from across the street,

MILLIE

I smell waves of meat and cheese. My nose quivers as the adults hurry inside behind the dog and girl. When the door closes, the meaty goodness drifting from the house disappears.

My stomach growls. I whine and tilt my nose to the sky and sniff for Big Guy. My sides constrict with something that feels sort of like hunger but is a different kind of emptiness. Big Guy and I were like a pack, like the family in the cozy house across the street.

Big Guy taught me everything I know about being a street dog—the safest time of day to hunt for food, where to find the best dumpsters, and how to be invisible. But one day, Big Guy went out to search for food and didn't come back. He just disappeared, and I don't know why.

Big Guy is the fastest, smartest dog I have ever known. His black fur conceals him at night. His blocky head and wide chest make him seem even larger than he already is. He didn't have puppies to slow him down. The dogcatcher could not catch him. We've been separated many times, by bad weather, by fences, once by a very long train, but he always finds me.

Always.

Except this time . . . he's been gone for many, many days.

And his scent is growing faint on the trees and shrubs and dumpsters around town.

Twitching my nose side to side, I inhale the frosty air for any sign of him . . . or danger. But the cold street is clear. It is late. Soon, the moon will drop behind the mountains that circle the city, which means I need to get back to the alley. Sticking to the deepest shadows, I trot toward the center of town where the buildings grow taller, where I hid my nest behind another row of trash cans at the back of a shop that makes many flavors of something warm and wonderful called *bread*.

Ducking my head, I push against the growing wind, then squeeze my eyes to slits. I must trust my nose to guide me home. But the air blows one way, then the other, confusing everything. My head jerks. Paper flaps in a clump of dead weeds on the side of the street. My lips close. My nostrils widen. That is not just any old piece of paper flapping in a clump of weeds. It is a food wrapper! And lots of times, where there is a food wrapper, there is human food.

My tail wags. My mouth floods with water. And I race over to the weeds. I snatch the slippery paper and gobble down a few bits of meat and bread sticking to it. Hungry for more, I rub my lips in the leftover grease, then pull the last morsel of food to the back of my throat. I will save it for when I return to the alley.

The dogcatcher can't get me there. I may be small, but I am smart and have planned many ways to escape if he tries.

And he will try.

He always tries.

But his noose will not tighten around my neck the way it did Mother's because I will not let my guard down. I will be careful, careful, careful. I will trust my nose to lead me through the icy night. I'll trust it to keep me and the tiny creature I've hidden in the alley safe too.

Chapter Two

When I finally slink into the alley, rats with beady eyes scamper into cracks and under buildings. They are just trying to survive, like me, but they are trouble. Rats make messes and steal food. And humans really, really do not like them.

Normally, I would chase them. Tonight, I'm too tired to even snarl. The bites of human food did not fill my belly. Plus, the tiny puppy in my nest needs me. I cannot risk swallowing or dropping the bit of food I am saving for her.

So I turn my head side to side, sniff for danger, and scrape my side along the brick wall. The bricks grab bits of my hair and scent and will remind rats and other animals to stay away. Flattening my head and shoulders to the ground, I crawl inside the big pipe that runs under the building. When I reach the nest, the puppy lifts her teeny white ears and whimpers.

A human dropped her near my trash cans a couple of days ago. I can barely find enough food to feed myself without Big Guy, but I couldn't leave her there to starve. I'll help her like Big Guy helped me until the weather warms and she's big enough to survive. Then she'll have to learn the ways of the street or find a family of her own. It's a decision all strays must make.

I don't mind street life. It's more predictable than family life. Not all families live in warm houses that smell like mountains of meat and cheese. Not every child is as happy as the bouncy girl with the ball on top of her hat. Believe me. I know. I had a family once. There are mean people in the world—just like there are mean dogs. People who will turn on you when you least expect. People who can't be trusted.

Standing very still, I lower my muzzle and offer my grease-soaked lips to the puppy, like Mother used to do for me. The pup's warm little tongue tickles my whiskers. I push the food I'm saving for her forward from the back of my throat and drop it in the nest at her paws. She grabs it, swallows it in one bite, then hungrily licks my lips, hoping for more. She's starving. But I have nothing more to share, so I nudge her toward the warmest spot at the back of the nest.

Little Pup scratches the cloth lining the nest, releasing the smell of the bread place I found it behind. The sugary goodness has mostly faded, but it still holds a whiff of the old man who works there and an even fainter hint of the young girl that belongs to him. Little Pup circles a few times, then collapses in a ball. Her eyes close. Her sides rise and fall like she's sleeping, but her little body shivers.

She has nothing but fuzz to keep her warm. Thankfully, I have a wiry topcoat to keep me dry and a soft furry undercoat to keep me warm. Lying in the ripped papers and soft cloth, I quietly wrap my body around the shivering pup. Tonight, my coat will keep us both warm.

Being a street dog has some rewards. I'm never left alone inside a fence. I'm never tied to a rope and dragged along a sidewalk. I can sniff whatever I want for as long as I want and

MILLIE

squat to relieve myself wherever I want. But street dogs have challenges too—the worst is the empty feeling inside that no amount of food, water, or rest ever seems to fill.

Thankfully, tomorrow is trash day! The day when humans push large cans full of soggy papers mixed with lots and lots of delicious food bits out to the sides of the road. On trash day, I rise early and check my favorite spots before the trashmen can steal the best food away. There's always some meat and cheese. Every once in a while, there's *chicken*.

Until then, I need to rest. So I lower my face to the puppy's. Instinctively, she snuggles closer. My nose and ears stay on alert even when I close my eyes. As the night grows colder, I drift in and out of sleep. The puppy's warm side rises and falls against mine.

When the stink of rotting meat and tiny biting insects pricks my nose, I startle. I'd know that smell anywhere. It's a large rat, *scritch-scratching* through the pipe leading to my nest. My body tenses, ready to pounce. The hair at the back of my neck rises. Lifting my lip, I growl deep in my chest but do not bark. I don't want to wake the pup.

The sneaky rat scurries back to where he came from. I rest my head near the puppy's face. Based on the way the rat was squealing, he should not return tonight.

Chapter Three

When the first speck of light peeks through the opening at the end of the pipe, I stand. My stiff legs ache. I slept in the same spot for too long. Now, not wanting to disturb Little Pup, I quietly stretch my neck and back. She stirs despite my effort to be quiet.

When her eyes open, she doesn't stand and burst into a flurry of motion like most pups. She is too weak. Thankfully, the rats are gone. They slithered back to their hiding places when the sun rose. This means I can bring Little Pup food and enjoy trash day.

A screeching *beep, beep, beep* sounds in the distance. The trashmen. They're going to beat me to the best cans if I don't hurry. So I bend low, rub my face against Little Pup's soft cheek, and try to tell her to stay put and not be afraid, that I will return for her. But my insides tighten, and my tail sags when I think of the last time Big Guy rubbed his cheek against mine. He did not return.

Bellycrawling away from the pup, I slink into the alley. Light seeps from the crack under the back door of the bread place. My stomach growls at the smell of the yummy goodness the old man bakes each morning. Frozen pavement bites my paw pads as I trot past the empty trash cans in the alley and onto the quiet street. The alley cans aren't like the ones that get wheeled out to the street. They are bigger, heavier, and sealed tight without anything easy to grab.

The street cans contain the greatest treasures and are worth venturing farther away. So I trot to the corner. When I reach the first set of cans, stretchy cords secure the lids, and there are not any bags on the ground near the cans either. My ears droop.

I'm starving, but the scent of something rich—cheese and eggs maybe—draws me up the street to the next set of cans. As I trot forward, my toenails *click-clack* in the silence. My nose quivers as I approach. A wonderful person must live here because these cans are overfull, with their lids leaning to the side like tilted hats.

Standing on my back legs, I press my front paws against the cold can. The lid wobbles, then crashes to the ground. My head jerks from one side to another, sniffing for any sign of humans. There is none. So I bounce on my hind legs over and over. I am an excellent jumper. At the top of each bounce, I nip the plastic bag that holds the trash. After several bounce-nip-bounce maneuvers, the bag tears, and a river of delicious food rushes to the ground. My tail wags my body.

Success!

I'm surrounded by papers soaked in food juices, strips of bread, and tiny scraps of meat. I would eat the food-soaked paper if I had to, but I do not have to. Today, there is enough food in this one can to feed me and Little Pup until *next* trash day—fish, meat, cheese—every yummy treat a dog could imagine. There's even a whole chicken with most of the meat still

attached! I rip it from the bones with my teeth, then lick my lips. It is so delicious; I cannot stop myself. I shove my whole muzzle inside its skeleton and lick and lick and lick the juices from the inside too.

I'm so absorbed in my magnificent meal that I do not smell the trash truck until it's practically on top of me. When I finally hear it, my face is buried so deep in the chicken skeleton I can't shake myself free. Lowering my head to the ground, I shake and shake, but I'm stuck like a mouse in a snake's jaws. Frantic, I paw and tug at my face until the chicken releases me, then I flick my head back and forth, searching for an escape from the trashmen. My heart pounds against my chest. My sides heave. I'd run for the alley, but I don't have food for the pup. I need to find another set of cans before I flee.

So I press as close as I can to the wall, slink forward, and try to avoid the skinny man hopping down from the back of the truck. He wears flat, dark pieces of glass over his eyes, which is very confusing.

When a dog's eyes go big and dark, he's on super alert, ready to fight or run. Other dogs know to be cautious around him. When humans wear those dark circles over their eyes, it's hard to tell if their eyes have gone big and dark or if it's just the strange circles covering their eyes.

"Hey there, little dog," the man coos like he's talking to a puppy. Then he reaches for the can near the tricky chicken and dumps its contents in the back of the truck.

I pause, my pads slick. He sounds nice enough. It might be safe to move past him. But humans are hard to understand, especially ones with scary dark circles over their eyes.

"Want a treat?" he asks as he places the can on the ground and reaches inside his pocket.

My head jerks. I know the word *treat*. It's supposed to mean tiny morsel of delicious food. But *treat* can also be used to lure dogs into cages or even into the dogcatcher's noose. I lift my lip at the man, trying to tell him I want to be left alone and that I really, really don't want to bite him.

"Come on, pooch." He smiles, squatting to my level and tossing his treat toward me but not close enough that I could snatch it without risk. "Blizzard's coming. You don't want to be out here alone tonight."

I show a few more of my teeth. I would never bite a human. He doesn't know that, though, and I'm desperate for space. I need him to back away.

The large man inside the truck lowers the glass near his face. "You can't save 'em all, Phil. Come on. It's freezing."

"You can try," the man on the street mumbles as he reaches for the next can.

I stand perfectly still, my tail clamped between my legs, ready to run if he steps toward me.

"They have to trust people if you're gonna help them." The man in the truck jabs his finger in the air. "That little flea bag looks like it wants to bite your face off."

I whine. If I don't move soon, the moisture leaking from my paws will freeze to the sidewalk and pin me in place.

The skinny man with the dark circles over his eyes reaches into his pocket again. "You're just scared, aren't you, pup? You don't want to bite my face off . . ." He tosses another treat on the ground, showing a mouth full of his own teeth, which is another

MILLIE

confusing thing about humans. They show their teeth when they're shouting and angry and when they're happy and smiling.

Flattening my ears against my skull, I crouch down. Just to be safe, I growl and snap my teeth in warning.

The man's smile drops. He shakes his head. "Suit yourself, little gremlin. You're gonna wish you had a warm home and a nice family to take care of you tonight."

When he turns to grab the next can, I dart forward and snatch his treats from the ground. Holding them carefully in my cheek, I run. My ears flap against my face like tree leaves in a thunderstorm.

I don't look back.

I run.

And run.

Back to the alley.

Like my life depends on it.

And maybe it does.

Chapter Four

Later the next day, fluffy bits of icy water called *snow* fall from the sky. And fall. And fall. Little Pup joins me in the alley behind the trash cans to lap up some of the melting bits of fluff, but it's too cold for her to stay out very long. So I nudge her back toward the pipe.

In a sudden burst of energy, she yips and bows, inviting me to play. I shove her a little more firmly with my nose. It's too cold for puppy games, and she needs to save her energy. She needs more than melted snow to fill her belly. She nips at my chest anyway, then crouches to the ground, her tail wagging her little body.

Snow tickles my whiskers, and I can't help myself. I wag, too, and roll her onto her back with my nose. She wiggles joyfully when the flakes land on her belly. Then she squirms to her feet and bumps me on the side of the neck with her nose. I copy her, falling on my side and rolling over like she knocked me down. I haven't had this much fun since I was still part of a pack with Mother, Brother, and Sister.

Big Guy didn't play like this. Ever.

MILLIE

Lost in our game, I don't notice the door of the bread place open or the girl step outside until she squeals.

"Puppies!" Her hands wave near her face. The icy wind whips her dark curls into a frenzy.

I recognize her voice and the sweet mixture of smells that make her who she is—bread and paper and the light sweat of a young human. I've seen and smelled her from a distance many times. Big Guy and I smelled her sitting on the back steps of the bread place with her papers last summer when we first slept in the alley. She's the one who left behind the sweet-smelling cloth I used to line the nest. She never noticed us before, which is the way it should be. If I hadn't been careless and distracted by Little Pup today, she probably never would have noticed me.

Now, Little Pup springs to her feet, scrambling toward the safety of the pipe. I freeze. My ears flatten. My pads moisten. My insides quake, but I stand my ground and bark, trying to look bigger and braver than I feel.

The girl doesn't seem to care.

"Pops! Pops! Come quick," she calls over her shoulder to the bread place. A smile stretches from one side of her face all the way to the other. Her dark eyes sparkle.

"What is it?" a voice rumbles as the door opens.

I don't wait around for another human to appear. I bolt for the pipe too.

They call for us and make friendly clicking noises with their mouths, but we do not budge from the nest. They even wave delicious cooked meats in front of the pipe. My mouth waters. My insides flutter. We still don't move.

They talk and talk, using so many words. The puppy whines like she wants to go to them. I turn sideways, blocking her escape.

"Can we keep them, Pops?" The girl's whine isn't all that different from the puppy's. "Please. Please. I'll take care of them."

"Tori, the health inspectors will shut down the bakery if they find a dog inside." The man breathes heavy when he speaks, like an old dog. "You know that."

"We could keep them in the apartment."

My ears lift, straining to understand their words, but they speak so fast, I can pick up only bits and pieces.

"We would need permission and money for a pet deposit. What we *can* do is call animal control—"

When the man's voice drops, I tilt my head, lift my ears, and strain to make out his words. It's hard to tell from this far away, with so many street and rat smells pushed together in the pipe, but I think he smells hurt or sad all of a sudden.

"But they'll—" The girl sucks in a big gulp of air.

"They'll take care of them, Tori." The old man's voice is firm, like Mother's bark.

"I know what happens to dogs at the shelter." The girl's voice drops even further.

Despite my excellent ears, I can barely hear her when she speaks. I inhale, trying to smell the feelings leaking from her small body. There's a whiff of fear, or maybe it's pain.

"What happens is they'll be given a safe, warm place to sleep and eat, and if they're deemed adoptable, they'll get transferred to a rescue organization or the Humane Society." He speaks more slowly now, with pauses between his words, the way humans sometimes speak to dogs.

"But—"

"But nothing. They'll be fine. If they're adoptable, they'll find a home."

The pup nudges my backside with her nose. I do not budge. I sense their words are important.

"What if they're not adoptable?" The girl's voice cracks.

"You said they're puppies—and small. The young, cute ones *always* get adopted."

"I'm not sure they were both puppies. One of them might have been older."

Little Pup nips my tail with her tiny, sharp teeth. I lift my lip in warning. Now is not the time for games.

"It's the only option, Tori."

My ears rise when a truck rumbles into the alley. A door opens and slams shut. Another human joins the old man and the young girl in the alley. But his loud truck drowns out all their voices and their smells.

Thankfully, after a short time, the truck rolls away. The humans leave. My nose twitches, eager to understand what the humans are up to. The alley outside the pipe seems to wait in cold silence for something big to happen too. My body shudders on high alert, also waiting for something big to happen.

But . . . nothing happens.

The human scents continue to fade. When I'm sure they're not coming back, I creep toward the opening at the end of the pipe. Little Pup follows close behind. A new smell pricks my nose. I seal my lips for a better sniff. My tail lifts, brushing the pipe above my back.

The aroma of tangy meat and sweet bread mixes with something metal. My mouth floods with water. Wary of a possible trap, I sniff carefully for any sign of danger, then slink from the pipe to the shadows of the trash cans. Little Pup tumbles out behind me, without any concern for rats, strange humans, or the lone coyote that's been prowling the edges of the city, and bumps into two bowls I've never seen before.

Without lifting an ear or twitching her nose, she shoves her face in one of the bowls. I flick my head one way and the other, then sniff carefully for anything unsafe. Satisfied that we are not in danger for now, I bury my face in the second bowl. Scents of the girl and her old man linger on the food, but the smell is faint as we smack and gobble the heaps of bread and meat they seem to have left just for us. I think they might be good dog people. They seem to understand our need for space because they've left us alone to eat and eat.

When our bellies grow tight, we drag ourselves back to the nest. Feeling full and warmed from the inside out, we sleep so soundly I don't even know if the rats sneak around us or not. We sleep until the sound of human voices wakes us the next morning.

"I just wish they would trust us."

It's the girl with the dark hair and the dark eyes.

"They don't know us, Tori."

"I know."

Their feet crunch the snow as they approach.

"And you know, from everything you've been through with your mother, how hard it is to reestablish trust."

"I know." Her voice sounds more like air than a human voice. "But I can wish. And Mama and I are making progress when we talk on the phone. You said so."

"You are, and I don't ever want you to quit hoping or wishing."

Their feet stop outside the pipe.

"But remember, these are dogs we're talking about—frightened strays that have been living on the streets. They don't speak our language. That makes it even harder."

A puff of human food smells tickles my nose.

"I know," she says.

It's meat. They've brought meat!

We creep forward for a better sniff. My mouth waters. Little Pup squirms behind me. I growl a warning. We must stay still inside the pipe and wait for them to leave. Little Pup whines, but we wait. And wait. And wait before I crawl to the end of the pipe and twitch my nose. When I'm sure they're gone, we slip out, and our paws sink into a layer of icy snow.

Little Pup jumps and bounces toward the end of the alley, making little yipping sounds each time her paws land in the icy sheet of white that covers the ground, the steps leading to the bread place, even the large trash cans. When a car swishes along the snowy street outside the alley, Little Pup skids to a stop, leaving a long puppy-wide track in the snow behind her.

I bark, and she races back. Our alley looks like a strange new land, but it mostly smells like our regular old alley, except for the yummy smell of human food. The bowls are back and filled with mounds of beautiful, wonderful, glorious meat—sausage maybe. Forgetting the snow, we suck down the food like air, then sneak to the end of the alley to survey the street together. A cold wind flaps my ears around my head. Little Pup bounces and wags beside me, but she shivers too.

The sides of the road and the sidewalks are covered in the same thin blanket of snow as the alley. Cars zip back and forth in the center, where the road is still clear. Now that we're fed, I don't have any reason to leave Little Pup in this freezing weather. So we head back to the nest with swollen bellies to stay warm and rest until the snow melts.

When we wake again, the now-familiar scent of meat and bread mixed with humans fills the air. Unlike the trashman with all his crouching and talking, these humans feed us and leave us alone, which is why we're less cautious when we venture to the end of the pipe to check the metal bowls for more meat.

It's also why I don't smell the man hidden behind the trash cans until his noose slides over my head. When it tightens around my neck, I yelp like a puppy.

Twisting and tugging with all my might, I try to yank free. I need to protect Little Pup. But it's no use. I'm trapped. Each time I yank, the noose grows tighter until I can't breathe. And when I can't breathe, I can't smell.

"Don't be so dramatic." The man drags me toward a large truck at the end of the alley. "You'll be fine."

My mouth opens to pant, but it's no use. My legs wobble. I need to squat. Little Pup whines from deep inside the pipe. Forcing my paws down through the snow to the pavement beneath, I fight until the skin around my nails begins to tear.

"Knock it—"

A shrill yowl pierces the air.

It might be Little Pup.

It might be the girl.

It might be me.

I can't be certain because the alley blurs, and my body sinks down, down, down into the icy snow.

Chapter Five

I wake to the smell of terrified dogs and metal bars pressed against my belly. My world is dark, but I know the feel of the truck rumbling beneath me. I pant. I drool. My pads drip water.

I'm caught—trapped. So much for all the practice hiding. So much for all the ways I planned to escape from the dogcatcher. So much for protecting Little Pup.

Closing my lips, I pull scent in through my nose. Smelling helps me focus and settle a little. My nostrils widen. Many, many dogs have been caged in this truck before me—most recently, a sick, old, girl dog. Her smell swirls with a cloud of other dogs in the back of my nose, but there's not even a hint of Little Pup. She's gone, and I fear she won't make it long on the street without me.

When the truck makes a sudden turn onto a bumpy road, I flatten my belly against the cold metal of the cage. A whine rises in my chest. Before my nose knows what's happening, the truck stops. The back opens. Despite the cloudy gray sky, my eyes squint, surprised by the sudden change from the pitch-black truck to daylight. The panting returns. My sides heave.

"Be nice," the dogcatcher growls. Thick leather gloves cover his hands and most of his arms. "We can do this the easy way or the hard way. Your choice."

I stretch my lips over my teeth and growl back at him. My body tenses when his large body leans over mine.

"Have it your way." He reaches in and grabs me by the back of the neck with one massive hand. With the other, he slips the noose back over my head. Then he plops me on the snowy pavement and drags me toward a squatty brick building. Inside, everything is cold, hard metal and tile. Cages filled with dogs line one wall. Some of the dogs smell sick. Some smell hungry. They all smell scared, and they bark so loud the building shakes around us.

I try to whine, but the noose traps the sound in my throat.

"Hush, dogs!" the man shouts as he shoves me into a bottom cage and slams the door.

Dogs still bark, but the building stops shaking.

"Jada will check on you later." He huffs, then turns out the lights and marches toward the door he just dragged me through. "I've got five more calls today, and the roads are getting real bad."

Curling into a tight ball, I crouch in the back of the cage, trying to hide and showing the other dogs I don't want any trouble. My neck stings where the noose gripped me. My insides ache. And for once, it's not with hunger.

The worst has happened. I lost Big Guy, just like I lost Mother, Brother, and Sister. I lost Little Pup. The humans got me. I have no way to escape, and I'm pretty sure these aren't the best humans. They're not the kind who understand dogs, not the kind who watch and listen and give us space like the old man and the young girl in the alley.

I think these might be bad humans—unpredictable ones who speak nice words one minute and offer food, then poke and prod and raise their voices the next. Like the *family* who took me in for a little bit before I became a smart street dog.

I haven't always distrusted humans the way I do now. After I lost Mother, Brother, and Sister, and before I found Big Guy, I actually thought I wanted people of my own and a home. From a distance, humans seem pretty amazing. A lot of dogs like them better than other dogs.

Not me. I learned the hard way. People and their families are unpredictable, especially the mom, dad, and boy who took me to their home when I was a pup. At first, the boy was happy when he found me in the woods near the park. He snuggled me against his warm chest and took me inside his warm house. The mom and dad fed me lots of good food. But after a while, they left me home alone more and more and got very, very angry when I had to squat inside the house. The boy wasn't always happy and snuggly either. Sometimes, he played too rough.

One time, the dad, who was always rushing in and out and was never around much, slammed my paw in the door. He didn't mean to, but it hurt. A lot. One of my toenails split. There was blood. Even though I tried very hard to lick it away, it stained the carpet. And the mom shouted. And shouted. I learned fast that humans care a lot about their carpets and protect them—almost like dogs protect their bones.

My ears flatten against my face. I have enough to worry about right now without thinking about that day when the dad hurt my paw, when the mom shouted about the carpets, and, worst of all, when the boy kept poking me with his toy stick. But I can't stop myself. I keep worrying about it.

That day, I whined and let my ears and eyes droop and tried to show the boy that I was too hurt to play. But he kept poking and making quick movements with his toy stick, like he wanted me to grab it.

"Get it. Get it!" He flicked my paw over and over.

I yelped, unable to stand the pain and begging him with my eyes to stop. My paw felt like it might burst.

Frustrated with me for not playing, he poked harder. I flinched. Then he moved in for another jab. I didn't know what else to do. I snapped at the stick with my teeth. Normally, I'm very good with my teeth. I know exactly how much pressure to apply to carry a puppy in my mouth without piercing its skin. I know when and where to nip when I play without harming even the tiniest kitten—not that I would ever play with a scratchy kitten.

But that day, I hurt so badly that I actually felt sickness in my belly. Somehow, my teeth scraped the boy's hand, and he screamed—a scream so loud and terrible, it sounded like he was being eaten by a wolf.

"What in the—" The mother raced into the room, hair flying and hands flapping around the boy, me, the stick.

The next thing I knew, she shoved me out the door with her foot and into the cold, dark backyard. I lay in the dirt under the deck and licked my wound, trying to stay very still. I must have fallen into a deep sleep because I didn't hear or smell the dad until he was pulling me from under the deck and into his car.

MILLIE

We went for a long ride. He opened the car window. Nice night smells billowed inside. I thought maybe this was his way of trying to make me feel better, but his face was all pinched up.

"I'm sorry, girl. We never should have brought you home." His voice was all choppy.

I scooted toward him. Even though my paw still throbbed, I managed to nuzzle my head under his hand. Humans seem to like resting their hands on dogs' heads. Their breathing usually slows, and the uneasy chemical smells on their breath usually lessen.

"You're not a bad dog. I don't think you meant to bite Mason. We're just not a good dog family—not right now anyway. Maybe we're supposed to be cat people. I don't know. All I know is Natalie will never let you stay after what happened tonight."

It was the first time I realized humans could form water in their eyes. I whimpered, trying to show him that I understood his sadness but also wondering why he said that terrible word *cat*.

We drove on and on in the darkness, with his hand resting on my head. The human smells of cars and gas and bricks faded away as the fresh scent of trees and forest creatures trickled in from outside.

"You're a cute little girl." He stroked my ears, and I sank further into the seat. "I promise someone will want you. Very rich people own the horse farms out here. Natalie says horse people keep terriers around their barns for rat control."

My eyes grew heavy from all the ear stroking. If the dad and I could spend more time alone together like this, I might be okay with the unpredictable nature of his family. Then, all of a sudden, he stopped the car and reached across me to open the door.

"It's time for you to find a good home." He unclipped my collar and waved toward the field outside. "Get out."

Tilting my head, I watched his face. My nose twitched at the lovely smell of the wide-open space and all the grass. But I didn't move. The humans always fussed if I tried to dart out a door or a fence.

The dad and I were finally getting to know each other. I didn't want to ruin that, so I sat perfectly still. Then he opened his door, stepped out, and came around to lean in through the door on my side.

"You'll be okay. You're scrappy." He scooped me against his chest and rubbed his face against mine. "Your paw is just bruised."

I licked his cheek and relaxed against his body, trying to show him that I liked this new dad very much. Then, before I knew what was happening, he placed me in the grass on the side of the road and drove away.

Just like that, everything changed again.

I've been getting by on my own ever since. I started by trying to build a nest in the barn near the place where the dad abandoned me, but that did not go well. An angry woman found me and aimed a loud stick at me that blasted me with some sort of fiery hot pebble. So I moved from one barn to the next, never staying in one place very long and moving closer and closer to the city until one day I smelled a dog much bigger than me and followed him all the way to the alley. He was so big and so strong. I figured he had to know something about taking care of himself, so I stayed with him to learn—that was Big Guy.

MILLIE

I've learned a lot since those days. I'm very good at getting by now, so I hunker down in the back of the cage and wait for an opportunity to escape this noisy building, the same way I escaped from that angry woman with the loud stick and escaped from the trap a man set who was very protective of his trash cans when I first arrived in the city.

But I wait and wait, and there's no opportunity to escape.

And if I don't escape soon, I fear I will be too late to save Little Pup.

Chapter Six

Several days and nights pass. Dogs and cleaning chemicals fill the place with loud sounds and sharp smells. The humans who come and go, like the woman named Jada, are very careful about closing every door and gate. There's no way to escape and not even the faintest whiff of Big Guy or Little Pup. Sometimes, I miss them so much, I can't even eat all the food Jada gives me.

I worry for Big Guy and Little Pup. Life as a stray is very dangerous. There are struggles like hunger, thirst, and sickness and dangers like men and women with traps and fiery sticks. But worst of all, there are fast cars—fast cars that slam into distracted dogs and toss their bodies to the side of the road and leave only the outside of their bodies behind, while the inside part of them that makes them a real dog goes somewhere else entirely.

Curling myself around my aching belly, I whimper for Big Guy and Little Pup. The more days that pass, the more likely it seems something bad has happened to them. I fear I might not exchange sniffs or play bows with either one of them ever again.

When the Jada woman pushes a cart loaded with food bowls toward my gate, I prick one ear and then the other, trying to make out the words she speaks beneath the earth-shaking barking of the hungry dogs lining both sides of the building. She slides a bowl of food under the gate at the front of my kennel, then reaches for a pile of cloths stacked in the bottom of the cart.

"I wish we could find you a home, little girl, before . . ." Her words trickle off like a drying stream in the heat of summer. Her dark eyes soften, almost like they will make water, but they don't.

I inch toward the bowl. She seems nice, but she's also the one who led me from the small cage in the back room to this kennel with a rope and no way to escape. There's a dog-sized door at the back of the kennel, but it never opens. And the coldest, tightest air I've ever smelled pushes through the cracks around it. If I don't lie too close to the little door, the kennel is warm enough though. The water is clean.

My stomach growls, and I lower my head to nibble at Jada's food. She opens the front gate and squeezes inside the kennel with me. My ears flick in her direction as she places a square of soft cloth in the corner.

"Stay warm, Little Girl." She squats and offers a soapy-smelling hand to me—the same hand that held me down when the man in the backroom shone his light in my eyes, poked inside my ears, and pricked me with something horrible that stung like a bee.

Shying away from her hand, I drop my tail and flatten my ears, begging her to just leave me alone.

"We'll be open for adoptions when the main road's cleared." Many long twists of hair swing gently around her face when she talks. "But you won't find a home until you let your guard down." She shakes her head like she's the one trapped in a cage, then stands and slips back out the way she came. The gate closes behind her with a snap as she pushes her cart to the next dog.

She and the dogcatcher have trapped each of us in separate kennels, but I still push my bowl under the soft cloth in the corner just in case a dog escapes and tries to steal it. The building quiets as the other dogs devour the last of Jada's food. The shaggy girl across from me lies on her cloth, her sides rising and falling quietly.

With no Little Pup to protect and no food to hunt, there's really nothing left to do but curl up on the cloth, rest, and watch for a chance to escape. Without the sun or moon to watch or even the coming and going of humans and cars, it's hard to know the time of day. Instead, I've learned to focus on the spreading and fading of Jada's scent as a way of knowing when to expect her again. When she delivers the morning bowls, her earthy, soapy fragrance falls and clings to walls, covers our cloths on the floor, even coats the fur of the other dogs. Then all the barking, tail wagging, and air seeping in from outside spread her scent particles apart. The smell of Jada mixes with the smell of other dogs and the building. When it dulls to the point that I have to twitch my nose to find it, I know it's about time for her to return with her cart and our next meal.

Every now and then, I close my lips, pull kennel air into my nose, and check for the loosening of Jada's smell. I do it now. It's still not time for her though, so I plop my head on the cloth that smells like her to wait some more.

Then, all of a sudden, the door at the end of the building whooshes open. Dogs stir. Some lift their heads. Others stand and pace. The puppy beside the old girl across from me jumps up and down, wags, and whines all at the same time. A few dogs bark low and deep.

I freeze. All I wanted was another meal and a chance to escape and to check on Little Pup and maybe find Big Guy. Instead, the scent of a stranger invades my nostrils, and strangers almost always mean pain or trouble. But there's nowhere to hide, so my jaws part. Panting, I slouch and slink to the back of the kennel.

I'm suddenly thankful for the whining puppy across the way. Maybe, if I'm very lucky, the stranger will head for the wiggly bundle of cuteness.

And.

Leave.

Me.

Alone.

Chapter Seven

A trickle of something new and lovely mixes with Jada's cloud scent as the two humans shuffle toward my kennel. It's a bouquet of grass, a very well-fed dog, and lots of something like dried sticks. And cheese! Shiny black hair, the shade of a moonless night, is tied back from the new woman's face, showing off calm, dark eyes. She moves slowly, like one of the wide streams crisscrossing the horse farms where the dad from my first family abandoned me. If I wanted a human, which I definitely do not, I think I might want one like her.

Jada and the stranger do not look at me. They squat and *ooh* and *aah* over the cute puppy. Exhaling, I release a whoosh of air from my nose.

"Puppies are like a fresh canvas. You can make them into whatever you want." Jada smiles at the pup, but her voice sounds tired as she wiggles her fingers through the kennel bars. The puppy licks and nibbles at her hand.

"They're cute." The other woman reaches through the bars and rubs the puppy behind its ears. Begging her to scratch its tummy, too, it flops to the ground, rolls on its back, and squirms adorably. "But so much work."

MILLIE

Tilting my head, I listen to the ring of this new woman's short, calm words. If all humans spoke like her, dogs would be much less confused by all the human chatter.

"I want an adult dog. Small. Friendly. Nonthreatening. A beagle or beagle mix maybe." Her eyes move to the older girl dog standing quietly in the next kennel. "Something her size. But younger. A dog with the energy and temperament to read quietly with kids at the Cherokee Youth Center one hour and perform trick dog demonstrations at the senior center the next."

"Huh," Jada grunts. "Don't ask for much, do you, Lee? You probably want it to be cute and housetrained too."

"Sure. And why don't you throw in minimal shedding?" The new woman smiles and lifts her shoulders. "May as well dream big. Right?" Her eyes move farther down the row of dogs. Then she turns to face me.

My body stiffens. I can't retreat any farther. My behind is already smashed against the cold wall behind me.

The woman steps toward my kennel. Then her body freezes like mine. She doesn't flash any teeth. Instead, she moves her eyes along my body without staring me directly in the eye.

"Uh-huh. Nope. No way." Jada places a stiff hand between the woman's face and my kennel. "You said you wanted a versatile dog with the confidence and temperament to go anywhere and do anything." Her voice rises higher with each word.

"What's her name?" The woman, whose name must be Lee, squats and offers her hand with the meaty, smelly side up, unlike most humans, who usually keep that best part balled up and hidden away.

MILLIE

I turn my head. I like the way she moves and speaks, but I am not—I repeat *am not*—trusting her or any other human that easily. I didn't even trust Big Guy at first.

"I haven't named her because I'm worried we might not place her." Jada shakes her head. "If we do, it will be in a quiet home—maybe with an older person who lives alone. I don't see her enjoying going to school or dog class with you and Bella."

My tail clamps further between my legs. The urge to squat tugs at my belly, but I'm not a puppy. I will not stoop that low in front of these humans.

"She might be aggressive, Lee."

The woman's head jerks toward Jada's face. "Has she bitten someone?"

"Well, no." Jada scratches her tilted head.

Lee turns back to me, her eyebrows squeezing together. "She's the perfect size—sturdy enough to stand her own with rowdy children, small enough to carry under my arm if I'm in a hurry."

Jada's long twists of hair swish when she shakes her head side to side. "She's a quaking mess of nervous energy. Jim said she snapped at him when he brought her in the other night. What about a nice little Papillon mix?" She waves her hand to the other end of the building.

"You and I both know most dogs snap and growl at the noose." Lee scratches her chin without taking her eyes off me. "People will love her—I think." She stands to her full height, like she's ready to leave or has made an important decision.

"What?" Jada's head swivels back and forth from Lee to me and back to Lee.

"They will. She's a border terrier. She won't shed. She's a wirehair. Her coat has to be hand stripped."

"You mean a border collie?" Jada's mouth hangs loosely, like she forgets to close it after she talks.

"No. A border terrier. They're super popular in Great Britain."

Jada's head cocks to the side. "Lee, I think you're making a mistake if you believe this dog can pass the therapy dog test and go to school with you like Bella."

My moist paws slip when I try shrinking further against the wall.

"If she's doesn't work out for me, she will have received a lot of socialization and good care and be more likely to transition smoothly to the quiet, one-person home you think is best." Lee pulls a short, thin rope from her pocket and releases a whiff of a friendly dog and a puff of cheesy goodness into the air. "And you won't have to feed her between now and then."

My body is too tense to wag, but my tail relaxes a little. Other than the rope, the woman respects my space *and* carries cheese in her pocket. As far as strangers go, she seems as good as it will get.

"Let me take her to the visitor room for a few minutes." She pushes the gate out of our way. "I trust Bella more than I trust myself when it comes to choosing a dog to rescue. She's had her shots, been spayed, microchipped, all that, right?"

"Yes, but . . ." Nervous chemicals seep from under Jada's arms and from behind her knees. "There are several other more confident dogs to choose from."

If I weren't concerned for my own safety right now, I'd worry more about Jada's hands and arms. She flaps them around like a bird with a broken wing when she speaks.

"This dog is special." The corners of Lee's mouth turn up. She shows just a hint of teeth, but they're not the bared threatening kind of teeth. They're the open-mouth-play-with-me teeth dogs show right before they drop into a play bow.

"They're all special, Lee."

I tilt my head to listen. Jada's normally confident voice is more air than words when she speaks now.

"But this little girl's a border terrier. I haven't seen one since I was a kid. My grandfather worked for a lady who raised them once. They're athletic, sturdy cuddlers."

I turn my head from one human to the other. They speak too fast now for me to pick up more than a word here or there. Then their voices grow serious, like two dogs sizing each other up before a confrontation.

"*That* is not a cuddler." Jada points a finger in my direction. "That's a scruffy pile of wiry hair with a beard."

Lee opens the gate and slips inside my kennel. "Isn't the beard adorable? Have you held her against your chest?"

"She won't even let me touch her." Jada's lips press together in a straight line. She rests a balled fist on her hip.

Lee carefully loops the short rope over my head. She doesn't squat to be closer to me or touch the top of my head or reach for my ears the way so many humans do. She just keeps her eyes on Jada when she talks. "They were bred to follow foxhounds in England, so they usually get along well with other dogs, which makes them unique as far as terriers go. The hounds were too big to chase the fox underground, so the hunters needed a smaller dog, brave enough to go underground and hold the fox face-to-face until the hunters could dig it out. They're the best of both worlds—brave enough to hunt, pack-oriented enough to snuggle at home with humans or other dogs."

Jada's eyes roll around in her head, almost like balls.

"Their skeletons are strong and flexible, too, which is why they're such good tunnellers." Lee's voice and eyes go soft at the same time. "If they trust you, their bodies will melt into your chest when you hold them."

"If someone in your dog training class were looking for a therapy dog prospect, would you recommend this dog?" Jada's hands finally stop flapping when she places them on her hips.

Lee's voice drops. "Maybe not, but have I ever picked a dog I couldn't train?"

"There was that black-and-white spaniel mix that bit you in the face."

Lee's hand flies to a stripe of tender-looking pink skin on her cheek. "That's not fair. That dog had a medical condition."

"A medical condition that almost cost *you* your eye."

They talk and talk and talk for so long without bothering me that I could almost forget to be afraid of them—but not quite.

"I won't take her if she's aggressive, Jada. Let's just let Bella spend a little time with her, okay?"

Lee pushes my gate open. She doesn't tug on the rope she placed around my neck. She doesn't look down to see what I'm going to do. She doesn't even speak to me. She just moves forward like a dog leading its pack through the forest. I'm so caught off guard by her unusual behavior.

I don't know what else to do.

So . . . I follow.

Chapter Eight

Before I know what's happening, Lee leads me into a large room dotted with a table, chairs, a box of toys, and a large dog with long yellow hair. As the heavy door *thunks* closed, Lee slides the rope off my neck. The wagging dog barrels toward us. I freeze as she slides to a stop at Lee's feet. For her size and age, she moves surprisingly fast.

"Well, hello, Bella!" Lee squats to rub her face against the dog's white, whiskered cheek.

Clearly, they belong to each other. They even share some of the same grass-stick-cheese smells. The dog seems very friendly—almost too friendly, if you ask me. So I stand still as a lamppost and wait to see if she likes dogs as much as she likes her human, but she barely seems to notice me. Her whole body wags for Lee. She licks Lee's face and hands. When she finally does turn to me, I lick the side of her mouth and let her sniff my muzzle to show respect for her age. I do not move when she circles around to my backside, trying to show her I don't want any trouble.

"So far, so good." Lee steps away from us and toward the empty chairs. The thick rope of black hair swishes against her back when she moves. "Want to talk about Bark in the Park for a few minutes while they socialize?"

Jada crosses her arms and plants her feet.

"Come on." Lee sits and pats the chair beside her. "How's the fundraising going?"

While they're distracted, I slink toward the safety of the table on the other side of the room. Bella noses through the box of toys. Her tail fans the scents of many dogs that have visited here before us.

"Not so great, but it's still early." Jada watches me when she speaks.

"I guess it's hard to get donors motivated when Mother Nature keeps acting like it's the dead of winter." Lee leans back and crosses one booted foot over the other.

"Lee, I really need to get back to work."

"Give Bella a few more minutes. Nobody's adopting a dog in this weather. Please." Lee clasps her hands together near her face.

Jada sighs and clomps across the room. "You're here."

My ears lift. My body tenses, but I stay put, hoping they will forget about me. Humans do that sometimes—completely forget dogs are around. The boy with the toy stick and his mom and dad forgot about me a lot.

"Come on. Five more minutes." Lee pats the empty chair again. "I'm always here to volunteer or foster."

"True." Jada sighs and plops down. "And we're very thankful." Her face softens when she smiles.

Without moving or taking in air, they watch as the yellow dog, whose name might be Bella, gently grabs a fluffy toy from the box and brings it to me. If it were just me and Bella in the

MILLIE

alley or in a forest, I might want to play with her. But here, my paw pads are too slippery and my mouth too dry to play chase or shake fake bunnies in my teeth.

Lying very still, I press deeper into the floor as Bella drops the yummy-smelling bunny at my paws, then lies beside me.

"Well, that's good enough for me." Lee's head bobs up and down. "Good girl, Bella. Good girl, Millie."

I can hear the smile in her voice even with my eyes focused on the floor.

"Millie?" Jada croaks like a frog. "You're giving her a name? Already?"

"Yep. Millie, short for Millicent—the woman my father worked for, who raised border terriers."

Jada's mouth hangs open like she might start panting. "I thought you valued my judgment with dogs."

"I do. She might not be the absolute best choice, but I have to trust my gut—and Bella's. And this might be my once-in-a-lifetime chance to rescue a border terrier." When Lee stands, she reaches in her pocket and pulls out a stick of cheese. "Here you go, Bella." She breaks off a bit of cheese and tosses it to Bella, who catches it from under the table before it hits the ground, which is pretty amazing. "Come on, ladies," she says and taps her leg.

Bella leaves me and the fake bunny to join Lee. Jada remains slumped in the chair like she's stuck there.

"Come on, Millie." Lee taps her leg again.

I think she's calling *me* Millie. I don't think I want a name, but if I have to have one for now, I guess *Millie* is better than *Mouse*, which is what the boy and his parents called me. *Mouse* is not a name. It's a tiny, less horrible version of a rat.

Lee throws a speck of cheese toward me. It lands under the table near my paws. I lick it and pull it into my mouth with my tongue but stay where I am, protected under the table.

"Good girl, Millie," she soothes and tosses me another bit.

I'm not sure why I'm a *good girl*, but I appreciate all the cheese. It's the first human food I've tasted in many days. And it is very, very delicious.

Bella wags, reminding Lee to share another bite with her, and Lee reaches in her pocket again and again. The cheese seems to flow from her like scraps from an overflowing trashcan, proving my gut was right. As far as people go, Lee is a good one. And Bella seems to be a good dog, too, because she doesn't rush over and grab my food the way most dogs would.

"Come on, Millie. Let's find you a home," Lee says as she bends and slips her rope around my neck.

My ears lift. My behind almost wags.

I know the word *home*.

My home is in the alley with Big Guy and Little Pup.

If they can, they will find me in the alley, and I will chase them.

And teach Big Guy to play fight like Little Pup.

And we will wrestle.

And mouth each other with our teeth.

And take turns pinning each other to the ground.

And frolic.

Like puppies.

Like family.

Chapter Nine

Lee and Jada lead me and Bella down a long hall to another room with windows, where I can see outside for the first time in many days. Drips of wet snow splat the ground beneath the trees. My paws itch for something—anything other than this hard, slick floor.

Lee and Jada sit across from each other in front of a box that makes electrical humming sounds. Bella rests on the floor while Jada pushes one paper after another to Lee. Distracted by a bird twittering about on a tree limb, I don't realize what's happening until Jada stands.

"You know I want what's best for you and for . . . Millie, right?" Jada sniffs and wipes at her eye, then steps toward Lee and wraps her arms around her. "And how much I appreciate you fostering and rehoming our dogs, right?"

"Absolutely, and you know how much I appreciate your advice, even if I didn't take it this time, right?"

Bella pops to her feet when Lee zips her jacket.

They move toward the door as one. I have no choice but to follow.

"I do." Jada nods, then calls after us. "Keep me posted, okay?"

"You know it." Lee pushes the door open.

Cold, fresh air whips my ears around my face. Bella bounces along the sidewalk and toward a car that smells like her and Lee. I bounce a little too—excited to go home and leave this place with all its cages and loud noise.

Inside the car, warm air blasts from narrow slits and tickles my whiskers. I prop my paws on the door handle, stand beside Bella, and peer out the window. When the car stops at a sign, Lee gives Bella a piece of cheese, then places a bit of cheese on the tip of her finger and offers it to me. I lick it into my mouth. For the first time in a long time, maybe since I was a pup in the nest, I feel warm on the inside and on the outside.

I could not rest in the kennel. I had to stay on alert at all times for an opportunity to escape and to make sure no other dogs tried to take my cloth or my bowl. Now my eyes grow heavy. My head grows heavy. It sinks lower and lower.

"Close your eyes, little Millie." Lee runs a hand down my back. "You're safe now."

Her smooth voice rolls over me like her hand down my back. I melt into the seat beside Bella's warm body.

When my eyes open, we're driving through a long, skinny hole in the side of a mountain.

Lee's hand rests on my side. "We're almost home, little girl."

There's that word again. *Home.*

But I do not smell home. I do not smell the bread place or trash cans or lots of cars. All I smell is dirt and trees and a few small forest creatures in the distance.

MILLIE

The sun glares down on us as we exit the side of the mountain and enter a whole new world. Snow lies in mounds on the sides of the roads and in the shade here, too, but there are also spots where the muddy ground peeks through the melting slush. The tall buildings of the city are gone. Now, small houses sit back from the road. Clumps of trees, empty fields, and melting snow fill the spaces between the houses.

Lee's car slows. We turn into a slushy driveway. Maybe this is where she will stop to open the door and let me out.

No. Her car drives right up to a tiny white house. When we do stop, Lee opens her door, steps out, and comes around to Bella's and my side. When she opens the door, Bella hops down to the ground and trots toward the house. But Lee steps in front of me before I can hop down, then slides her thin rope over my head and gives me another bit of cheese.

"Good girl, Millie. Let's go." She pats her leg and follows Bella without waiting to see what I will do.

I have no choice, so I follow Lee and Bella up a set of stairs and into a warm house that smells like flowers and cheese and dried sticks—just like Lee and Bella. Lee slips the rope off my head, and Bella trots into another room that smells like mounds and mounds of food. I don't move. My last experience inside a house did not go well. I don't know whether to sniff or hide, so I just cower near the couch.

"You're such a good girl, Bella," Lee says as she follows Bella into the other room. "You're gonna help me train Millie, aren't you?"

My lips tingle at the sound of dog food clicking and clattering into a metal bowl. My mouth waters. I haven't eaten a full meal since the old man and the young girl left bowls of meat and bread in the alley for me and Little Pup.

"Come on, Millie! You ready to eat?"

My ears perk.

More dog food clatters. Bella crunches and snuffles. Inching forward, I peek through the door.

"Good girl, Millie. Yes." Lee places a bowl of food on the floor near me. "Bella's a sweet girl." Bella's tail wags, but she doesn't lift her massive head from her bowl. "But she will eat your food eventually if you don't."

I glance at Bella's white face. She doesn't look at me. She just lifts an ear.

I creep to the bowl and gulp mouthfuls of food in case she decides she wants mine too. She does not, or at least she pretends not to. She just sighs, shuffles over to Lee, and plops down on the floor to stretch out like a frog so her belly can rest on the cool wood floor. I'd be hot in this house, too, if I had that much hair.

As I suck down the last of my food, Lee runs her foot along Bella's side. My paws grow slick on the floor. Now that I'm finished eating, I don't know whether to stay frozen in place where I am or scurry under a table or chair to watch them from a safe distance. So I stay put until Lee collects our bowls and places them on the counter. When she heads to a door that opens at the back of the house, Bella scrambles to her feet surprisingly fast. Her hairy paws slip and slide as she scuffles to the door. My head and tail droop, but I follow.

Outside the door is a large fenced yard. Bella trots from one melting pile of snow to another, pausing a few times to squat and mark along the fence line. At the very back of the yard, she squats again to do her big business.

I race around the yard, looking for an escape, but the gates are locked tight. So I find the shadiest corner of the yard, do my business, and watch Bella. Following Big Guy helped me survive the streets when I came to the city alone. Following Bella might help me survive here.

"Good potty. Yes," Lee calls.

As we trot toward the house, she gives us each a tiny treat. It is tiny, but it is meat!

That night, Bella and Lee climb into a human bed together to sleep. Lee pats the soft blankets for me to join them. I don't move. I should not be here. I'm a street dog. I should be prowling the night for food.

"Come on. You can do it, Millie." She pats the bed again.

Bella's tail thumps the bed.

I whine. Humans care even more about their beds than their carpets. The family that took me home before shouted if I jumped on their couches or chairs, but Bella is on this bed. So I stand on my back legs and carefully rest my front legs on the side of the bed to better examine it.

"Good girl, Millie. Yes." Lee pats the bed again.

Bella thumps her tail, but I cannot join them. Lee seems like the smartest kind of dog person ever, but I barely know her. If I'm wrong and she isn't asking me to join her and Bella on the bed, she could shout at me for trying or, worse, pull out some horrid contraption like the dogcatcher's noose or the banging sticks some humans use to fire hot rocks at dogs and other animals. Playing it safe, I circle and scratch until I've pawed a warm spot on the rug beside the bed.

"Suit yourself, little one." Lee presses a thin stick on a lamp, and the room goes dark.

I lie awake most of the night, worrying about Little Pup and listening for sounds of nightlife. But there are no passing cars or scritch-scratching rats here. There's only the occasional sound of the wind rustling a bare limb against the house.

It's so eerily quiet, I barely sleep. When the sun finally brightens the window, Lee stirs under the covers and Bella hops down to greet me. As soon as her paws hit the floor, her tail wags her body.

I met a long-haired yellow dog like her once before when Big Guy and I ventured into a neighborhood for trash. Its tail constantly wagged its body too. Maybe that's what all long-haired yellow dogs do—they wag, wag, wag.

Kind of like I watch, watch, watch.

Right now.

And always.

Chapter Ten

The next days with Bella and Lee pass quickly. Their routine becomes more predictable, which is nice. Last night, I bravely hopped into bed with them. Today, I feel more rested and less on guard, which is nice too. My fear of this new place and of Lee lashing out in anger if I misunderstand her wishes melts more and more each day, just like the snow outside. Lee rises before the sun to care for us. She feeds us and takes us to the grassy backyard. She throws a bouncy ball for Bella. Bella brings it back every single time and never gets tired of doing the same thing over and over.

Every once in a while, Lee throws the ball to me. I do not bring it back though. I am a hunter, like Mother, not a dog like Bella, who picks up strange things like ducks and balls and even papers and carries them to humans in her mouth without biting into them. When I grab the ball, I shake it like a rat in my jaws and run with it to the grassiest spot in the center of the yard, then lie down and chew it.

After we play in the backyard each morning, Lee takes us inside and hides hard rubber toys packed with treats around the house—under the couch, behind a door—then leaves for most of the day. Bella and I find the toys and eat and chew until the sun rises above the house.

Most days, Bella lies in a spot of sun near the front door. At first, I paced and paced and paced around the house, feeling trapped and worried about Little Pup. But I learned it's no use. There's no way to escape. I've looked everywhere.

One day, I tried digging in the couch. Another day, I tried chewing something called a basket, which is made of the dried sticks Lee enjoys twisting back and forth. Even though baskets smell delicious and are made of sticks, they are apparently not for chewing.

It doesn't matter what I do though. Bella is always there. If I dig in the couch, she bumps me with her nose. If I attack a basket, she clamps it firmly in her mouth and stands there until I let go. If I hide, panting under the table, she stretches out beside me. When I'm not pacing or panting, we lie in a sunny spot together.

One day, a strange man in a hat left a box on the front porch, and my tail clamped between my legs. I hid under the kitchen table and barked. And barked. And barked. I might be learning to trust that Lee will not react in anger, but I will never feel that way about strangers who drive loud trucks and wear hats.

The days grow longer and warmer. When the sun begins to drop each day, Lee returns. She still smells like me and Bella and dried sticks and fresh air, but she also smells like gobs and gobs of children and cleaning chemicals.

Sometimes, we sit with her on the porch while she twists and turns the dried sticks she collects into the baskets she loves. Bella stretches out along the top step. She watches the gate at the end of the driveway, ready to greet any human or animal that might wander up to the house. I prefer the safer spot behind Lee's chair, where I can rest and think about Little Pup and Big Guy.

Other times, Lee brings out something called a *rake*, which is even better than the brush she drags through her own hair. My wiry coat doesn't shed like most dogs. It gets itchy if I don't scrape it regularly along bricks or tree bark. Now I can lie on my side and let Lee do all the work for me. Each stroke of her rake pulls out clumps of old hair and polishes my coat until it shines like morning sunrays on a shallow puddle. It feels wonderful, sort of like being groomed by Mother as a pup. Maybe even better because the rake removes more hair than mother's tongue ever could. In fact, it removes a mound of hair so large that it looks like there's another dog my size and color lying on the porch beside me.

One evening, I drift in and out of sleep, lazy from my recent meal and full belly. When a car rumbles up the driveway, I startle and scramble to my feet. Lee raises a hand and smiles. Bella's tail thumps the porch. My tail stiffens. I stretch my neck to peek around Lee's chair. Then I bark and bark and bark, trying to tell them to be on guard—that strange cars mean strange people, and strange people are scary.

"Shhhh, Millie. You're okay. It's just David." Lee stands and places her basket in the seat of her chair.

The car rolls to a stop beside the porch. A tall man, who must be David, steps out. A hat disguises his eyes.

"Evening, Immokalee." He nods his head at her. Sun glints on his white teeth. He grips a bunch of flowers in one hand.

Lee's eyebrows rise on her face. She smiles but does not speak. I growl at David's hidden face, but he does not back down.

"What's so funny?" he asks and clomps up the steps and onto the porch.

"Nothing. You're just the only person who calls me Immokalee." She tilts her head and smiles but does nothing to protect herself from the large man. "It's nice."

"Your Cherokee name is beautiful." His deep voice sounds over my high-pitched bark.

I curl my lip and bark higher and louder.

"Who's the little one hiding behind the chair?" David waves his free hand in my direction. He offers the flowers in his other hand to Lee.

"Shh, Millie." Lee stares me directly in the eyes, like she's trying to remind me she's the boss, then turns back to David.

I whine. A growl forms deep in my chest. Clamping my jaw, I try very hard not to bark.

"For me?" Lee takes the flowers from David's outstretched hand. "To what do I owe the great honor?"

Bella steps forward and nuzzles her head under David's free hand. The hair on my shoulders stands up.

"Good girl, Bella." He rubs his hand down her neck, and she does nothing to stop him. She likes it. She likes being out in the open and unprotected. "My yard's exploding with them. So . . ." His shoulders rise and fall.

Lee presses her nose to the flowers. David leans down and offers his cheek to Bella. She licks him. The urge to squat grips my behind, but I will not wet the porch like a scared puppy in

MILLIE

front of Lee and this man. My sides heave as I cower behind her chair, not wanting to be close to David or his hat.

"Seriously, what brings you so far out this way?" Lee lowers the flowers and studies his face.

"I needed to check Grandma Wachacha's roof after all that snow."

"Want to come inside?" she asks.

David's hand sweeps toward the mountains. "And give up this view?" He exhales and lowers himself to the porch step beside Bella. "No, thanks."

"Make yourself comfortable, then." She steps toward the door. "I'm gonna put these in water."

I stand frozen in place, not sure if I'm safer back here behind Lee's chair or if it's safer to cross the porch and follow her. So I do nothing but growl, trying to tell David to give me my space and leave me alone.

"Am I safe out here with her?" He points a finger at me and flashes his teeth.

"She's not aggressive—just scared." Lee's face softens.

"Doesn't fear make dogs aggressive?"

"I prefer the term *reactive*." She turns back to the man, her face serious.

"Right. You told me that." His head droops a little. "Reactive it is."

"Thanks." She laughs softly, then turns and slips inside the house, leaving me alone with Bella and this stranger.

I keep my eyes on him, but he doesn't reach for me or speak. He just stares off into the distance until Lee returns.

"Good job." The door creaks behind Lee when she steps back onto the porch. She hands David a glass of water and a small bowl of meat and cheese. "You ignored her."

"I always do what you say. You know your dogs." Studying the bowl, his eyebrows squeeze together. "Um, no, thanks." He pushes the bowl back toward her.

"It's not for you. We're going to treat the dogs while we visit."

"You know I'm a terrible dog trainer." His shoulders drop.

"We're not training. Just treating." She laughs. "I need Millie to learn that new experiences are good. Right now, her go-to coping mechanism is to run and hide or bark and growl. That's no way for her . . ." Her voice trails off. Then she shakes her head, smiles, and looks deeply into David's eyes. "It's no way for any of us to live. So when I take her new places, like the craft store or the park, I give her lots of treats."

David holds her eyes with his own, then shakes his head and laughs. "I'd like to be trained like that."

"We're not training, exactly, more reconditioning. We just happen to be sharing treats and building positive experiences with Millie while you and I visit." Her eyes narrow when she looks at him. "Will you take off your hat?"

"My hat?"

"Hats, sunglasses, all that stuff make the human outline look not quite right to a dog. I don't know her backstory. I think she's been a stray all her life or abandoned as a puppy. She definitely hasn't been exposed to much of the human world."

David removes his hat. He looks less threatening. His eyes are dark but just dark like a friendly dog's, not dark because they're enlarged and he wants to fight.

MILLIE

"Are you keeping her? Or fostering her?" His head turns in my direction, but he doesn't look me directly in the eye. "She doesn't seem super adoptable."

"If she were super adoptable, she wouldn't need me." The corners of Lee's mouth lift with her shoulders. "Give Bella a tiny treat. Then toss one to Millie—close enough that she has to stretch to get it."

Amazingly, David tosses meat toward Bella. She catches it in the air. Then he tosses a piece to me. I inch forward, snatch it from the porch, then dart back to safety behind Lee's chair. She grabs her basket, sits down, and goes back to winding more twiggy strips together, which always seems to make her smile.

"Is it for the arts festival?" David's hand jerks toward the basket.

I jump at the sudden movement. My heart slams against my chest.

Lee glances from the man to me and back to him. "No. It's for the Bark in the Park fundraiser. Remember, slow movements. Calm voice."

They speak words and more words, and my heart settles back inside my chest. Bella flops down on the porch and waits for David to throw her more food. When he finally does, I don't cower behind Lee's chair. I take a small step forward and wait for my own.

He and Lee talk and talk and talk.

He throws treat after treat—just like Lee did the first time I met her, when her treats flowed like water in a river.

"See if she'll take a piece from your hand." Lee stops twisting her sticks and watches.

David holds a piece of cheese in his fingers and offers it to Bella. She steps forward to take it. Then he offers me a piece. I stretch my neck, wanting to step forward too.

"Good girl, Millie. Yes," Lee says.

Lee seems to understand me more and more each day. My tail twitches at her words. I'm learning those words always mean something good will follow. Sometimes they mean it's okay to jump on the bed. Sometimes they mean Lee's gentle hand on my back. Most of the time, they mean lots of treats.

I take another step.

"Good girl, Millie. Yes." She smiles.

Her voice and those words urge me forward. Before I know what's happening, I'm nibbling the food from David's hand. He sits very still and smiles.

"Good girl, Millie. Yes!" Lee squirms like a puppy struggling to sit still. "Oh my gosh, David! That's the jackpot. Give her lots of treats."

David hands me one treat, then another, and another.

"I'm so proud of her! And you, David." Lee leaves her chair to sit beside him on the steps and wraps him in her arms. Nervous, excited smells seep from his hands and behind his knees, like he enjoys being squeezed in her arms.

Lee leans back to smile at me, Bella, and David. "This is a big step for her, even if she had to be coaxed. I think every new interaction is going to get easier and easier if everyone does as well as you just did with her."

Bella's body wags like something wonderful is happening. Lee and David smile so wide I can see all their teeth.

"She might be ready to go to school with me and meet the kids." Lee bounces up and down on her backside and wraps her arms around David again.

Bella's tail thumps the porch like the word *school* is the most wonderful of all the human words. David smiles over Lee's shoulder. They laugh, as happy as young dogs on a chilly morning. Their playfulness wakes something deep inside of me that hasn't stirred since I was a pup, or maybe since that snowy day in the alley with Little Pup. My tail moves side to side all by itself.

Confused, I circle again and again trying to catch it with my teeth. Lee and David laugh and laugh. Bella wags and bounces, and I realize that's what my tail is doing too.

Wagging.

And wagging.

Chapter Eleven

I forget all about the word *school* until days later when Lee clips collars around my neck and Bella's. When the boy with the toy stick first placed a collar around my neck so long ago, I tried and tried to shake myself loose. I learned it's impossible, though, and also learned that once you've had it on for a while, you almost forget it's there. Unless you get an itch beneath it, which doesn't happen too often if the human clips it correctly.

By the time Lee pulls her car into a parking lot that smells like many, many children, I've completely forgotten about the collar. In front of a large building, long lines of ginormous cars that Lee calls *buses* spew clouds of smoky gasses that prick my nose.

Bella's tail wags so hard it thumps against my face and the car door and back again. The tags on our collars jingle. Thankfully, Lee comes around to our side with ropes and releases us. Bella practically floats above the pavement as streams of children make their way into the large building.

"Bella!" they squeal from beneath the large bags they carry on their backs.

She prances for them and yips like a puppy.

MILLIE

Overwhelmed by all the sights and smells, I clamp my tail between my legs. I pant. My paw pads moisten.

"Ms. Berry, you have another dog," a child calls from the sidewalk.

"I do. She's a little uncertain about meeting new people. I'll introduce you later, okay?" Lee leads us away from the packs of children and toward a smaller door on the side of the building.

"Okay." The child waves and hurries to catch up with the other children.

Inside the building, several adults speak to Lee. I'm too overwhelmed by the smells of eggs, bacon, and bread floating from a large, noisy room packed with the most children I've ever seen in one place to try to understand any of their words. Away from the loud room with all the food and all the children, the school place smells like paper, books, and cleaning supplies.

Bella smiles and nuzzles her head under every hand that comes within reach. She's so big and so friendly, she mostly distracts the strange humans from bothering me, which I appreciate. I follow her and Lee from one noisy hallway to another, freezing and quivering behind them each time they stop to speak to someone new. Finally, we make our way down a long hallway lined with doors that open into large rooms filled with many tables and chairs.

Children of every shape, size, and smell fill the rooms. Some smell sweet, like donuts and cookies. Some are smoky like meat and cheese. Others are earthy like beans and peppers. They all smell wonderful. I might enjoy sitting near them and sniffing their scent clouds if they weren't so busy, busy, busy.

At the end of the hall, we enter a room that is smaller than the rest. A woman stands over a group of children seated at tables. She and the children turn to stare when we enter. Their mouths open, but before they can speak, Lee holds a finger to her lips. Soft air shushes from her lips. The children settle.

"This is my new friend, Millie." Lee bends down and unclips Bella's rope. "Thanks for covering for me, Ms. Patel. Getting out of the house with a new dog always takes a few extra minutes."

"Anytime." The woman, who must be Ms. Patel, nods. "We love helping the new pups prepare for forever homes. Don't we, friends?"

"Yes!" a boy with hair as light as Little Pup's leans over his desk to smile at me and Bella.

I stiffen. Bella prances from one child to the next.

"Ms. Berry!" A girl with waves of dark curly hair raises her hand in the air.

"Yes, Tori?" Lee bends down, runs one slow hand along my back, and holds out a tiny bit of cheese.

"I . . . I think I know that dog."

Lee glances from me to the girl and back again. "I picked her up at the shelter a couple weeks ago."

"My pops called animal rescue about two dogs in the alley behind our bakery a while back." The girl's face droops when she talks. "One of them had a beard like her."

"Millie was brought to the shelter alone. I asked." Lee's eyes narrow when she looks at me.

"The other one was a puppy. Our neighbor took her." The girl's eyes slide from the tip of my nose to the tip of my tail. "Can I pet her?"

"I'm sure everyone will be okay with letting you pet her first since you seem to have met her before. Right, class?"

The young heads bob together. When the curly-haired girl moves, she releases a scent cloud of warm bread and soap.

I know that smell. I know her! It's the girl from the alley.

She squats in front of me and offers her hand.

I pause, lower my head, and sniff deep and long. She smells wonderful. My nose tells me to go to her. My body tells me to be careful, but I can't stop myself. Underneath the perfume of bread and soap hides another scent that draws me forward.

It's Little Pup, and she smells bigger and stronger than before.

My tail wags a bit. All by itself. Despite my slippery paws, I take a tiny step toward the girl.

"Oh my gosh, Tori!" Lee laughs. "She never approaches anyone like that. Not even me. She definitely knows you."

"I knew it. It's her, Ms. Berry—the dog from my alley." The girl, whose name must be Tori, is not as busy as the other children. She does not reach over me to pat the top of my head like so many humans. Instead, she runs a gentle hand along the side of my face—kind of like I rubbed my face along Little Pup's the last time I saw her.

I inhale deeply. A bouquet of bread, the alley, and Little Pup fills my nose. Finally, I'm getting somewhere. A fast car did not get Little Pup, and if a fast car didn't get her, maybe just maybe, Big Guy is out there somewhere too. Maybe if I wag and nuzzle like Bella, this small girl with the waves of curly hair will take me back to the alley.

And back to Little Pup.

Chapter Twelve

Later, when a loud bell rings in the hallway, Ms. Patel peeks her head inside the room.

Lee waves at her, then turns to the children. "Push your chairs under, friends. I'll see you after P.E."

Tori and the others file out of the room with Ms. Patel and close the door behind them. Tori does not take me with her to find Little Pup. She leaves me closed in the room with Bella, Lee, and all the tables and chairs. Standing near the door, I wait and wait for Tori to return with the scent of Little Pup hanging on her clothes. But she does not return, so I slump to the floor, feeling like I've lost Little Pup all over again.

Bella rests her head on her paws near Lee's desk. Lee shuffles mountains of paper, and I twitch my nose over and over, waiting for Tori to return. But she still does not return.

When the sun finally rises high above the school, Lee takes me and Bella down the long hall and out a door to a patch of grass near many parked cars. There is no sign of Tori out here, so I do my business quickly. I do not want to miss her if she reappears.

MILLIE

Thankfully, Bella also does her business quickly. Then Lee leads us directly back to the small room laced with Tori's fading scent. I am breathing her in deep and long when an ear-piercing bell rings, and I startle. My breath catches. I freeze.

A tangle of loud voices breaks the silence after the bell. Before I realize what is happening, Ms. Patel leads the children back to us. They tumble around the room, sweaty and bumping and nudging one another like restless young dogs. My tail swishes like it wants to wag but isn't quite sure.

Lee bends down and opens a small cage on the floor beside her desk. The cage smells like many dogs but none of them Little Pup. The only thing in the room that smells like Little Pup is Tori. I whine to be near her, but Lee throws a small piece of chicken in the cage and says, "Kennel up."

This means I must enter the cage, which isn't so bad with Lee. She lines the bottom with a soft blanket that smells like her and Bella and always places treats inside. She never leaves me in the cage for too long either. It actually feels kind of safe in there, but today, I want to be close to Tori. I want to breathe in the scent of her and Little Pup, but I also have a new desire to please Lee. She has been working really hard to feed and care for me, so I lower my head and slink inside.

"Good girl, Millie. Yes!" She clicks the gate on the front of the kennel closed behind me. When I turn around to face her, she gives me another tiny bit of chicken. "Be a good girl and relax while we read. Then it will be almost time to go home. Okay?"

I let my eyes sag, hoping she understands I don't want to be in here for very long—that I need to be near the girl, that Tori is the one who can take me home to the alley and to Little Pup.

Lee is very smart, but she doesn't seem to understand my saggy eyes because she turns away from me to watch the children scurry from their desks to the floor at the front of the room. They giggle and chatter along the way.

"Why does she have to go in the kennel?" A boy who smells like rubber balls and fresh air points at my cage.

"So that she and I can both relax. She's not in trouble. I just need to make sure she's safe while I read to you all. I don't want her to wander off and get scared or get into trouble. Until I know she's comfortable with us, I need to watch her every second to make sure I set her up for success. Plus, she feels protected in her comfy place, without so many bright lights and loud noises." Lee pulls a book from a shelf near her desk.

"It's like Erik going to the regulation room to calm down," a boy with hair and eyes the color of a moonless night says.

"Exactly, Koa! Millie needs quiet time to rest in her crate just like Erik sometimes needs a few minutes in the regulation room to help him relax and focus." Lee pulls a chair that rocks back and forth to the front of the room and sits down.

Bella wags for the children then plops down between Lee's chair and my kennel. I rest my head on my paws but do not close my eyes. I want to see and smell what will happen next.

Lee raises her eyebrows and glances from one child to the next. "I'll read . . . when you get situated . . . and silent." She uses many pauses between her words when she speaks to the children.

Whatever is about to happen must be wonderful because the children suddenly sit perfectly still and do not make a peep.

Lee opens the book, stares into each of the children's eyes, then leans forward. "Now, where did we leave off yesterday?"

Many hands shoot into the air.

"I know. I know. Page one hundred and two." The boy with the almost-white hair twists when he speaks.

"Very nice, Erik. We were on page one hundred and two of *The Miraculous Journey of Edward Tulane*. But you know I care more about what was happening in the story than the actual page number. Good readers constantly make predictions about what will happen next when they read. They also summarize what they read regularly, even if they don't realize they're doing it. Who can summarize what was happening when we stopped on page one hundred and two yesterday?"

I do not understand all of Lee's words, but there is one that seems important because she and the children keep repeating it: *read*. It seems to have something to do with the book Lee holds very carefully on her lap.

Tori raises her hand and leans forward, releasing a wave of Little Pup smells. "The dog, Lucy, found Edward, the China rabbit, in a trash pile and took him to his friend Bull."

"Excellent, Tori. I love the way you used the characters' names when you summarized. Does anyone else have any important details to add?" Lee's eyes examine each of the children's faces.

The boy with the night-colored hair and eyes raises his hand.

"Yes, Koa?"

"Umm . . . Edward said that thing you liked about . . . having a rush of pleasure at being recognized . . . at being known."

"And what did that line about being recognized and known make you all think about?" Lee's chair creaks when she leans back.

Erik rocks side to side like he cannot sit still. "It made me think about how everyone in here knows my name but not everyone in my big classes does."

"Which do you like better?" Lee pushes off with her feet. The creaky chair leans back again.

Erik bites his bottom lip and rocks and rocks. "I like it in here, where everybody knows me."

"Me too," says Lee. "I think most people prefer places where they are recognized and seen. Don't you?"

Several children nod their heads.

Tori raises her hand. Her face pinches a little, like she's uncomfortable. "I agree with Erik. It's nice that we all know each other. But it's also like Bull said, 'It's better to be lost together than to be lost alone.'"

"Yes, Tori. I love that line too. It's definitely better to be lost together than alone." Lee rocks back in her chair and smiles. "So, let's be lost together with Edward while we read, okay, friends?"

"Okay."

"Yes!"

"Read. Please." A girl in back bounces on her knees.

"Okay. Okay." Lee runs a finger along one of the papers inside the book. "Here we go: 'Edward knew what it was like to say over and over again the names of those you had left behind. He knew what it was like to miss someone. And so he listened. And in his listening, his heart opened wide and then wider still.'"

Lee goes on and on. Her words run together one after another. This might be the most words I've heard her or any other person use all together. My eyes grow heavy. Bella's sides rise and fall in front of my warm, cozy cage.

MILLIE

It seems safe to rest. The children don't seem to be going anywhere for now. My sides relax. My breathing slows. When my eyes close, I dream of Big Guy and a field of clover. We trot side by side, sniffing the air for rabbits. In the distance, a small girl with waves of black curls and large brown eyes calls to me. "Millie, over here. Millie!"

Big Guy and I break into a run. Our bodies stretch and flatten like galloping horses. When we reach the girl, she offers us bowls of chicken. We devour the delicious meat. Warmed by the sun on our backs and the food in our bellies, we lie beside her on a soft blanket spread over even softer clover.

Then a loud ringing splits the air. I jerk to attention. My head whacks the top of the small cage. My heart pounds against my chest. Standing with my head pressed against the top of the cage, I sniff for Lee and Bella, for a clue as to what is happening. Lee and Bella are here. I smell them, but they're blocked from my view by a stream of excited children standing and scurrying to the back of the room. They're not just going to stand at the door in a line either. They're laughing and grabbing bags and jackets, like they're leaving for good.

I whimper.

They are leaving.

The children are leaving and taking Tori away.

That means they're taking the hope of Little Pup away too.

And there is nothing I can do to stop them.

Chapter Thirteen

Worried the children might not ever return, I whine and scratch at the kennel. I need to follow the stream of children exiting the room—need to follow Tori so I can find my way back to Little Pup—but Lee does not understand.

"You're okay, Millie." She smiles down at me, then turns to speak to someone at the back of the room.

It's Tori! She stayed. My tail swishes.

Bella walks to her and pushes her head beneath Tori's hand. My lips seal shut. My tail stiffens. Bella is wonderful, but I suddenly feel irritated with her—almost like she's trying to take away a bone or something that belongs to me. But that does not make sense. Tori does not belong to me. She is not a bone. I've never had a human of my own. But suddenly, I feel possessive of this girl with the big brown eyes, who smells sweet, like bread and Little Pup.

"You ready for some one-on-one reading time?" Lee steps toward Tori, rubs her hands together, then pats Tori on the back.

There's that word again—*reading*—and they both seem very serious about it.

MILLIE

Tori nods.

"What's it going to be today? *Pax*? *The One and Only Ivan*?"

"Can we finish the *Who Was* book about Anne Frank?" The corners of Tori's mouth turn up when she glances down at me.

My tail thumps the plastic cage. Each time it wags, I notice a growing warmth inside of me. If I'm not careful, my tail is going to take control of me instead of the other way around. For now, I let it wag, and I enjoy the smell of Tori and Little Pup.

"Of course." Lee's head tilts to the side. Her eyes narrow when she glances from Tori to me and back to Tori. "I think she's wagging her tail at you, Tori."

Tori's shoulders rise and fall. She smiles. "Dogs like me. I wish I could have one."

"Why can't you?"

"Pops says they're too expensive. But I think he's more worried we'll track dog hair into the bakery and ruin one of his perfect health inspections."

"Hmmm." Lee rubs her chin. "Why don't you grab the Anne Frank book. I'm going to open Millie's kennel. Remember, we're not going to reach for her or touch her unless she comes to us. In fact, let's don't even look at her, okay?"

"Okay." Tori turns her back and starts to walk away.

My wagging stops. My body droops.

Lee bends over, opens my cage, then follows Tori to sit at one of the children's desks. Tori slides into a seat beside her and opens the book. This book has a dark-haired girl on the front, not all that different from Tori. Lee and Tori do not look at me or talk to me, which is very unusual for humans. Usually, humans can't leave dogs alone.

Stretching my neck, I inch forward. It's the first time since I was a tiny pup that I do not feel the need to escape when a human opens a door.

Today, I choose to stay.

In this room.

I choose to stay here with Bella, Lee, and Tori.

If Big Guy and Little Pup were here, I might be very happy to stay in this room like this forever.

Chapter Fourteen

Tori and Lee sit side by side and take turns pointing and dragging their fingers along the inside of the book that seems so important to them. They say many, many words—too many words for me to keep track of. Sometimes, they stop and make funny *buh* and *cuh* sounds that seem to have something to do with the words and papers.

Bella lies near the door, watching people come and go in the hall outside the room. Her tail occasionally thumps the floor. When none of them are watching, I step quietly out of the cage and toward Lee and Tori. My paw pads moisten. My head droops, but I press forward.

When I reach what feels like safety under their table, my sides relax. My breathing slows.

"In spite of ev-er-y-th-ing . . ." Tori's words start and stop more often than Lee's words.

"Yes! *In spite of everything*!" Lee sounds excited, like she does before she gives me a bit of cheese, but she does not reach for her pocket and does not give Tori a tiny bit of cheese.

I crouch to the floor and very carefully lay my head on top of Tori's delicious-smelling shoe.

"In spite of everything, I still bee-leeve pee-pull are reel-ee . . . good at heart." Tori exhales like she's trotting up a hill, not like she's speaking words from a book.

Lee claps her hands and bounces a little, like something wonderful is happening. "Yes. *In spite of everything, I still believe people are really good at heart.* Look at you, Tori. You're reading an important and difficult book. That is one of Anne Frank's most famous quotations. I knew you could do it."

"I couldn't have done it without you and Pops." I hear the smile in Tori's voice even though I cannot see her face from under the table. "I didn't think I would ever be able to read that book."

"You did it, and isn't it beautiful? A thirteen-year-old girl who can still see the goodness in people, even after all the horrible things she saw and heard happening to the people around her."

"Anne reminds me of my grandfather. He always sees the best in everyone." Tori reaches under the table and brushes her hand along my neck and back.

I melt into the floor. Her next words rustle like air, so soft I can barely hear them.

"Pops even sees the best in my mama."

"He is a good man." Lee peeks under the table and meets my eyes. "You're a lucky girl, Tori. And you truly have a way with dogs." She points under the table at me. "I was really worried about bringing Millie to school. My friend at the animal rescue thought she might be aggressive." Lee scoots her chair back from the table. "Let's sit on the floor with her and see what she does."

"Okay." Tori gently pushes her chair back too.

Bella lifts her head like she might come join us. Instead, she thumps the floor with her tail and drops her head down to watch the hallway.

Tori's foot slides out from under my head as she and Lee join me on the floor. Not wanting to lose the scent of Little Pup, I crawl to Tori and rest my head in her lap the way I've seen Bella do with many adults and children.

Tori slides an arm under me. My body flinches. I go stiff as a fencepost.

"Oh! Wait—" Lee reaches for me, her eyes wide.

But before she can interfere, Tori pulls me to her chest. When she does, my nose brushes her long, curly hair. I inhale all the wonderful smells tangled there. Her heart thumps gently against mine. The tightness in my body loosens. My head rests naturally in the crook between Tori's neck and shoulder, almost the way I fit perfectly against Mother's side in the nest.

Tori's chest rises and falls like Mother's, too, and I melt further into her arms and body.

She laughs. "It's like holding a baby, Ms. Berry."

"I know, right? It's a border terrier thing." Lee's eyes sparkle like she's lit up from the inside. "They only do that with people when they're very comfortable. I guess I don't have to worry about her being aggressive." Lee shows all her teeth when she smiles. "Not with you anyway."

"I think she was just scared." Tori burrows her head against mine.

Lee's lips part, then close, then open again. "You sound like a dog trainer. How did you know that?"

Tori's shoulder lifts, pushing my head against her neck. "I just know how I used to get in trouble when I first moved here."

Lee nods. The light in her eyes dims.

"Remember, you told Ms. Jacobson I was scared. You said once I got over being scared, I would quit picking fights and getting in trouble."

"I remember." Lee's words crack, like they're stuck in her throat.

My ears lift and turn. I sniff but do not lift my head from the crook in Tori's shoulder. Lee does not smell sick. There is no reason for her words to stick in her throat.

"Well, you were right. Once I got over being scared, I quit fighting and getting in trouble." Tori runs a small hand down the length of my neck and back.

"I know." Lee brushes her eyes with her hand. Her eyes might be making water. I can't be sure, though, because she keeps blocking my view when she pinches the top of her nose. "And look at you now—reading like a pro."

"Yep." Tori nuzzles her head against mine again. "And writing a little too."

"Really?" Lee's voice rises as she drags out the word.

"Just some poems. I might let you read them sometime." Tori's voice drops, which is very confusing.

Dogs usually copy each other's behaviors. If one dog bows, the other bows. If one barks or wags, the other does too. Not so much with people.

"I would love that." Lee sits very still, like she doesn't want to scare Tori away, which is also very strange because Lee and Tori like each other very much and are not scared of each other.

Tori shakes her head and scratches me behind my ears. "I love Pops, but he works so much. I wish I had a sister or a brother or"—she smiles—"a Millie."

Lee rubs her chin when she stares at Tori. "Maybe Pops would bring you to a couple dog classes, even if he won't let you have a dog right now. I was going to swing by Sweet Treats tomorrow anyway after my Saturday errands. Want me to ask him?"

"Yes!"

Bella wags at Tori from across the room, then prances toward us. Lee bends over and wraps her arms around Bella's neck. They rub cheeks. I exhale and melt further into Tori's chest. It's almost like we're a pack of close-knit dogs in a den.

It feels really nice.

So nice, I don't want it to end.

happy humming sounds in the back of her throat and taps the wheel she grips with her thumbs. I stick my head out the window but do not wag my tongue like Bella.

The buildings grow taller, and the trees grow smaller on this side of the mountain. We pass the turn to school. There are more trash cans on the side of the road here and more cars. I know where we're going. To the city! Maybe to my alley! I wag my tail, hoping Lee will speed up, but she does not speed up. She turns the car into a parking lot and stops under a large tree in front of an even larger building.

"I'm just grabbing my library holds, ladies. I'll be right back." She opens her door and steps out. The breeze blows her dark hair around her face as she scurries toward the building.

Bella wags for her. I stand motionless, waiting to see what will happen next. Thankfully, Lee returns very quickly. She carries a stack of books so tall I can barely see her dark eyes twinkling above them.

"Quick, right?" The corners of her eyes crinkle when she opens one of the back doors and slides the books onto the seat.

Bella's tail whacks the seat, the door, my face, like she hasn't seen Lee for many seasons. She flashes her human-like smile as Lee slips onto the seat beside me. I swish for Lee one time. She looks into my eyes and smiles, like she understands that one swish of my tail means as much as all of Bella's.

"Good girl, Millie." She lowers her face to mine.

I touch my cheek to hers.

She starts the car again, and we're off. Bella and I wiggle back into our positions at the window to sniff. Many more humans live and work here than in the country around Lee's

Chapter Fifteen

But it does end. The nice bread man from the alley com[es] and even though I bark and whine and try to tell him not to t[ake] Tori away, he does. Then Lee loops a rope around my neck [and] one around Bella's and leads us away from the empty schoo[l.]

Despite the warm breeze on my fur and all the green pl[ants] coming back to life, I do not feel like prancing beside Bella[.] I drag my paws. I do not want to ride back through the hol[e in] the mountain and away from Tori, but I do not have a ch[oice.] Lee puts me and Bella in the car and drives us to her little w[hite] house.

I mope from one room to the other and barely eat my [eve]ning meal.

"Goodness, what a sad face," Lee says in the morning w[hen] she places my next meal on the floor. I mope some more [as] the sun rises high above the house. Then Lee loads us int[o the] car again and drives back through the mountain. We've [done] this so many times now I no longer quake with fear whe[n the] world blinks: light, dark, light. On the other side of the m[oun]tain, the air bursts with plant and animal smells that have [been] hidden beneath cold air and cold snow all winter. Lee m[akes] house. There are also many places here that cook large amounts of human food and smell delicious.

I'm so focused on the greasy, glorious smell of cooking meat that I don't recognize the sweet scent of the bread place until the car is stopping on the street in front of it. Then my mouth waters, and my body quivers. The bread place definitely means Tori. I hope it also means Little Pup and maybe even Big Guy.

I feel hopeful about Little Pup since I smelled her healthy scent on Tori's clothes. And feeling hopeful about Little Pup has also renewed my hope about Big Guy. More and more, I find myself whining for him. He's the biggest, strongest, smartest dog I've ever known. If any dog could avoid run-ins with cars or trips to the back room at the shelter, where many dogs go and leave the outside of their bodies behind, it's Big Guy.

"We're here, ladies," Lee says when she comes around to our side to let us out.

We jump down to the sun-warmed pavement. Bella wags for a man on the sidewalk. I don't wag. I don't whine. I'm not excited like Bella or frightened by the strange man like I used to be. I'm too focused on this street right now to care about a strange human.

I know these evenly spaced trees. I know the clumps of shredded wood piled in circles around them. I know the cracked sidewalk under my paws. My nose twitches. I tug toward a familiar smell drifting from the dirt and shredded wood under the nearest tree.

It's Little Pup. My tail wags my body.

I bounce like Bella.

"You're certainly in a better mood." Lee smiles down at me.

My body wags harder. My lips seal to better take in scent through my nose. Little Pup has squatted here recently, and she smells bigger, stronger, healthier, and like lots and lots of human food. My nostrils widen. My head flicks from side to side. I don't see her though, and I can't track her because her scent is everywhere—zigging and zagging one way, then the other, then crossing over itself. And it's all fresh, almost like she lives here. But how could she live here on the street and also smell like a house dog all at once?

I lock my legs, refusing to move, despite Lee's pressure on the rope.

Then she taps her leg. "Come on, Millie." She gives several short tug, tug, tugs instead of one steady, gentle pull.

I have no choice, so I drop my head and follow. Thankfully, we head for the bread place. The doors are propped open. I smell Tori and the man she calls Pops and their sweet bread. Maybe Tori will lead me to Little Pup if Lee won't. Bella presses forward.

"Uh-uh, Bella. No dogs allowed."

Bella lifts one ear, then the other, obviously confused by Lee's firm voice. I whine, too, uncertain why we've approached the place that smells so delicious but aren't allowed to enter. This is all wrong. We should not be leaving Little Pup's scent behind, and if we must, we should be entering the wonderful bread place to see Tori, not waiting outside.

Standing behind a counter inside, Pops wears a long white cloth over his human clothes. It's tied around his neck and waist with thin rope. A young woman with a messy pile of hair on top of her head talks to him and hands him bits of paper.

"Pops," Lee calls to them through the open door. "Will you tell Tori I'm here?"

He smiles, waves, and places the papers in the drawer of a beeping machine.

"Thanks." The young woman grabs what must be a bag of sweet bread and a cup of the hot brown liquid humans love so much and heads our way. "Cute pups," she says as she passes.

"Thanks." Lee nods and pulls us to a small table and chair on the sidewalk near the door.

Bella collapses on the pavement with a sigh and rests her head on her paws to watch the street. I sniff the legs of Lee's chair for signs of Little Pup. Then footsteps slap the ground.

It's Tori. She wears short pants that show her thin legs and open shoes held to her feet with straps of stiff cloth. Dark curls swish around her face, stirring up a wonderful bouquet of bread and books and fresh air.

Bella springs to her feet. I crouch a little and drop my head but do not retreat. I want to go to her like Bella, but Bella has pushed in front of me and is nose-bumping Tori's hand. So I stand there frozen in place.

"Hi, Ms. Berry. Hi, Bella." Tori laughs as Bella shoves her head under Tori's hand. "Hello, Silly Millie." She does not reach for me. She just quietly sits on the sidewalk beside me.

She is the perfect size. She does not tower over me, but she is big enough and old enough that she has outgrown the quick, unpredictable movements of puppies and tiny humans. I step toward her.

"Will you hold them while I get your books?" Lee hands our ropes to Tori.

"Sure." She rests the handful of rope in her lap, then runs her free hand down my neck and back.

The tightness in my belly unknots. Feeling brave, I step up onto her bare legs and give a slow wag. I barely notice when a young man, also wearing strappy shoes, walks past us and into the bread place.

"You are a cutie pie." She scratches me under the chin. "I love your little beard."

"Isn't it adorable?" Lee returns from the car bent under the weight of her books. "I've been brushing her every night and using a special rake to pull out all those clumps of dead, wiry hair."

"I wish I could have her." Tori lifts me gently to her chest and buries her face in my coat. "I'm the one who found her."

This time, my body does not tense. Instead, I snuggle into her neck and her waves of curls.

"You would be great with her." Lee smiles, then shakes her head. "But that's not why I'm here. I brought books—books for you to read with Pops and books for you to read by yourself."

"Okay." Tori's voice drops.

The short word that is supposed to mean something good drags out of her mouth like maybe it means something else today.

Lee slides books onto the tiny table, sits down, then removes one from the middle of the stack. "Since you've been writing poetry, I brought you something new." She holds up the book and runs her hand gently across the front. "They're called novels in verse, and I love them. They have fewer words on each page because they're written in stanzas. All the white space on the page makes them easier on the eyes too." She takes the ropes from Tori's lap and carefully hands over the book, like it's a tender piece of chicken. "This one is about a girl and her dog. It's called *Rez Dogs*. Joseph Bruchac is one of my favorite authors.

If you can read the nonfiction book about Anne Frank with me, you can totally read this by yourself."

"Okay." Tori takes the book and places it on the sidewalk beside her. "Thanks."

"You want to see what I've been teaching her?" Lee nods at me and reaches into her pocket.

Tori nuzzles her face against mine, then gently places me on the sidewalk beside the book. "Sure."

"These aren't the kind of advanced tricks Bella does." Lee pulls cheese from her pocket. "Come here, Bella."

Bella's body wiggles side to side. She steps forward, resting her head in Lee's lap. If she were smaller, I think she would crawl into Lee's lap and never leave.

"Bella, wait." Lee places a small chunk of cheese on Bella's nose.

I whine.

Bella just stands there without dropping or eating the cheese. It's harder for her than she pretends, though, because water drips from the side of her mouth like she really, really wants to eat the cheese.

"Okay." Lee nods, and Bella flicks the cheese into the air, catches it in her mouth, and swallows it without chewing.

Tori claps her hands softly near her face, like Bella is the smartest, bravest dog in the world.

"Millie's tricks are more about learning how to learn than they are about showing off. Her tricks require her to move her body in order to get the cheese, and that movement helps her relax."

"Okay." Tori watches intently, like something great is about to happen.

Lee reaches into her pocket for more cheese.

My belly growls.

"Let's trade." She hands Bella's rope to Tori. "Millie, come." She tugs me gently forward, then lowers a piece of cheese so close to my nose that I can almost lick it. "Spin," she says and moves the cheese slowly away from my nose and around to my backside.

Now *my* mouth waters, so I twist my body and follow the cheese.

"Yes!" Lee says when my head is back near her legs, where it started, and offers me a tiny bit of cheese.

"Now twist." She slowly drags the piece of cheese around in the other direction.

My nose follows the cheese toward my tail until my whole body is back to where it started.

"Yes!"

And just like that, Lee hands over another piece of cheese.

Lee's cheese fills my belly. Her joy fills something bigger inside of me, and my tail wags.

"It's called *luring*. It's the easiest way to train a dog. Without realizing it, Millie is learning to follow my hand and my words. Each time she gets a treat, she's learning how the game of learning works. She's learning that the word *yes* means she's going to get a reward. Eventually, I can use that word paired with a reward to start capturing behaviors I like and want her to repeat. Want to try it?"

"Sure." Tori hands over Bella's rope again.

Lee hands Tori mine and several small chunks of cheese from her pocket.

"Spin." Tori leads me around toward my tail with the cheese.

MILLIE

I lick my lips and follow.

"Yes." She hands over the cheese when my head is back where it started.

Bella wags her tail like she would really like to play follow the cheese, too, but it's my turn.

"Twist." Tori leads me around the other way with the cheese. "Yes," she says, when I'm back where I started.

And I get another piece of cheese. It is a wonderful game, way better than holding cheese on my nose like Bella.

"Excellent." Lee points from me to Tori. "You're a natural. I know it seems really easy, but usually the first time I show someone how to teach their dog to spin, they move the cheese too quickly. The dog gets confused and just stands there or turns the wrong way, looking for the cheese. But you took your time, read Millie's body language, and moved slowly enough for her to follow but with enough momentum that she had to move until she made it all the way around the circle. Do it again."

"Okay."

It's amazing. Tori leads me one way and then the other with the cheese, and every single time, I get to eat it.

"I'm teaching a Canine Good Citizen class next week. It's nothing fancy, just basic manners for dogs. If your pops will let you, you could work with Millie for me while I'm teaching the class. I think it would be great for both—"

The young man in the strappy shoes exits the bread place and interrupts Lee's words. He smells strong and calm and like several dogs of his own. Before I realize what's happening, he reaches down to pet me.

"What a cute dog." He scratches me behind the ears. "What is she?"

He smells so good I forget to growl or cower away. In fact, my insides warm a little. It's like my insides have learned that every time they meet a new human, they're getting meat or cheese or some other amazing treat. And sure enough, as Bella steps between me and the man and nuzzles her head under his hand, Lee feeds me many small bites of cheese.

"You're beautiful too." The man runs his fingers through Bella's long hair and smiles.

"The little one's a border terrier. The big one, demanding your attention, is a golden retriever." Lee hands me another tiny piece of cheese, just like every other time we meet a new person on the street or at a store.

"Can I give them a piece of my cinnamon roll?" The man's face rises hopefully.

"If it's tiny." Lee laughs. "They've already had a ton of cheese today."

The man reaches into his crinkly paper bag, releasing a wave of sugary goodness, then offers each of us a tiny bit of the bread. It is not meat, but it melts on my tongue. My tail wags. It might be the best thing I have ever tasted other than chicken.

Lee shakes her head as the man walks away, but her smile stretches from one side of her face to the other. "I am so proud of this little dog." She reaches to touch the side of my face. "I can't believe how far she's come. If you help, she might be ready for the Bark in the Park adoption day, and I could foster another dog that needs more intense training."

"She's so sweet." Tori scratches my belly. "What if someone adopts her and mistreats her?"

"The shelter does a really good job with screening families and matching dogs with the right temperament to the right home. And they have a policy to take dogs back without asking questions. It's hard, but I've learned to trust that most people are basically good at heart and want what's best for their dogs."

Tori's eyes narrow. Her head tilts like she's really thinking about Lee's words. "That's what Anne Frank said, 'In spite of everything, I still believe people are really good at heart.'"

"Yep. It's exactly what Anne said." Lee wipes her hands on her pants, pushes her chair back, and stands. The breeze picks up again, rustling the leaves above our heads. "Will you stay with the dogs while I talk to Pops?"

"Of course." Tori pulls me onto her lap with one hand and scratches Bella behind the ear with her other.

Bella plops in a heap on the sidewalk and lays her big head on Tori's leg as Lee gathers up the books and heads through the open doors and into the bread place.

My eyes grow a little heavy. It's the middle part of the day when Bella and I would normally lie in the sunny spot near the front window and sleep. My head sinks to Tori's leg beside Bella's. My eyes shut as I sniff in Tori's comforting smell.

Then the air shifts, moving the street smells one way and then the other. My lips seal. My head snaps to attention. I jump to my paws.

I smell Little Pup, and it's not the smell of her on Tori's clothes. It's not the smell of her squatting in the shredded wood under the trees either.

It's the real her.

She's here.

Now!

Chapter Sixteen

I jump to my feet. My nails click the sidewalk. My body wiggles. My nose knows. It's Little Pup, and she's rushing toward us on a rope beside a man and a boy. And she smells wonderfully well fed!

The man is huge. He limps, which causes him to lean sideways when he moves. The boy is about the size of the boy with the toy stick, who caused me so much trouble when I was Little Pup's age. This boy squints at a small, flat machine gripped in his hands, then jerks to attention when his toe catches on a crack in the sidewalk. His eyes lock on me, but I'm too focused on Little Pup to growl or hide. She jumps, yips, spins, and tugs on the rope attached to her neck.

Ignoring the boy, I wag some more and pull toward Little Pup as well. Bella and Tori stand to follow me. Little Pup tugs so hard her front feet leave the ground. She hops on her back feet and coughs.

"Hey! Stop that, Skittles." The large man snaps the rope but continues toward us. "You're going to choke yourself."

Little Pup squeals. My whole body wags harder. I bark and tug, too, until we touch noses, then inhale the smell of her clean fur. She bows to play, fake charges my chest, and nips at my paws. I should freeze and flick my head away to remind her how to respectfully greet an older dog, but I can't. She smells so wonderful, and she's here—alive and healthy. She could tear at my ears, and it wouldn't matter.

When she flops to the ground, I lower my head to sniff her belly. I bounce around her, paws tapping the pavement like another pup instead of a top, older dog. She can't stay still either. She wiggles, springs to her feet, and nips the sensitive corner of my mouth. I yelp and glance at Bella for help. But Bella just stands to the side, watching for Lee as if Little Pup and I do not exist.

"Easy, Skittles." Tori tries to step between us.

Little Pup jumps to lick Tori's face too. When she does, her rope tangles with mine and pulls down on my neck. She is not the tiny, weak puppy I remember. In fact, she is a bit out of control, almost wild. This happens sometimes when a pup doesn't have sisters or brothers in the nest to show her how to play politely. In the nest, a rough puppy will be ignored, nipped with sharp teeth, or even pinned to the ground when she plays too rough by her littermates. Little Pup did not learn those lessons, and if she does not learn some manners fast, she's going to get herself into trouble with humans and with other dogs—maybe even get herself hurt.

Despite the rope pulling down on my neck, I stand tall and still, trying to show her how to behave.

"Sorry." The man bends down, lifts her with one hand, and pulls her to his chest. "I don't know what we're going to do with her."

MILLIE

My ears droop. A whine squeaks in the back of my throat. I don't want Little Pup to leave, but I am a little relieved she's not nipping at my lips or bumping me with her head any longer. I wag for her to spread my scent around and to remind her I'm still here.

Tori smiles at the man and the boy. The boy smiles hesitantly then lifts his small, flat machine to his face.

I don't hear Lee step out of the bread place until she speaks.

"Hi, who's this?" She nods at Little Pup as she approaches but doesn't reach to pet her the way most humans do when they meet a small, cute dog.

Bella nudges Lee's hand with her nose, reminding her that she's there and not to pay too much attention to the cute puppy.

"It's Skittles." Tori reaches over to scratch Little Pup, who might now be called Skittles, behind the ears.

Little Pup squirms, wags, and whines all at the same time. The huge man adjusts his grip on her.

"She's the pup I saw in the alley with Millie before animal rescue picked her up."

Despite Little Pup's behavior, I wag and inhale the healthy smell of her floating down to the ground. She is definitely a house dog now. She smells more like this man, boy, and the inside of a house than she does the bricks and trash cans of the alley.

She struggles in the man's arms. He bends like he's going to let her down, but she jumps free halfway to the ground, landing on her face with a *thwack*. That doesn't slow her down though. She springs right to her feet, shakes off the fall, then lunges toward me and Tori and Lee and Bella. I want to rush toward her, too, but force myself to stay still. When she jumps on Lee's leg again and again, Lee crosses her arms, flicks her head away like a top dog, and ignores her.

"My name's Lee Berry." Lee lifts her hand to the large man.

"She's my teacher." Tori squats down to pet me. "And a dog trainer."

"Really?" The large man's eyes lift on his face. Even the boy's eyes lift from his machine, as if Tori's words are the most interesting words ever. "We could use a little help with this one." He scoops Little Pup from the ground again. It's almost as if the only way he can control her is if she's gripped firmly in his arms.

"I can see that." The corners of Lee's mouth turn up when she speaks. "I teach a Canine Good Citizen class—it's like basic manners for puppies and dogs—starting Wednesday at seven at the community center on Sixteenth Street. I have room for another dog. If she's up-to-date on her shots and you'd like to join us, it's $120."

Pricking my ears, I wag for Little Pup, reminding her how happy I am to see her, even if her human has to hold her.

"We'll be there, right, Ethan?" The man nudges the boy with his elbow.

The boy nods and rests a hand on Little Pup's back. She twists and wiggles to lick his fingers.

"Yeah, if it will help her." He rubs his face to her cheek.

She stops moving for the first time since I've seen her, like she really, really wants to please this boy.

I prick my ears and wag harder, thankful she and the boy care about each other and thankful she is healthy, safe, and living near the alley where I can find her again. I'm very relieved she has nice humans to care for her—that I'm not the only one looking out for her.

The man nods. "We better get our cinnamon rolls before Sweet Treats sells out."

"I'll hold her while you get the food." The boy slips his machine into the side of his short pants and pulls Little Pup to him.

"You'll see them too." Lee rests a hand on Tori's shoulder. "Because your pops said you could help with Millie while I'm teaching the class."

"Yay!" Tori bounces up and down, like Bella when Lee brings out the ball.

But I do not see a ball anywhere.

Lee reaches for Bella's and my ropes. "Now I need to get home and make some calls about Bark in the Park. We're adding art and writing contests this year." She nudges Tori with her arm.

"My poems aren't that good. I can't spell." Tori rubs my ears, then presses her lips to the top of Bella's head.

Bella smiles and swishes her tail.

"Spelling's an easy fix, Tori. It's what's up here that matters." Lee taps herself on the top of her head and smiles.

Tori's foot scuffs the sidewalk.

"Just think about it." Lee gently pulls me and Bella toward her car and waves. "See y'all Wednesday at seven."

My ears sag. Glancing over my shoulder, I watch Tori, hoping she will come with us, but she does not. My body slumps. My tail droops. A puppyish whine escapes my lips. Little Pup isn't coming either. Lee is a good dog woman. She is the top dog here, so I must follow.

But I do not have to like it.

If I were top dog, I would find a way for all of us to stay together.

Forever.

Chapter Seventeen

The next time Lee loads me and Bella into the car and drives us to school, my tail wags. I'm not sure whether it's school or Tori, but my tail does that more and more often now. Every time Tori enters the room, the healthy smell of Little Pup and sweet bread soaks her clothes. Sometimes, my tail even swishes for other children and adults at school but never for the man who pushes a bristly stick along the floors and wears a dark hat pulled low over his gray hair and gray face.

Bella wags for him, but she wags for everyone. Yesterday, Lee smelled exhausted as she shuffled mountains of paper at her desk. Bella rested near the door, ready to greet any passing children or visitors. She smiled at the man when he pushed his horrid stick beside her and mumbled something about *dogs creating messes and not belonging at school.*

Bella didn't bark or growl. I tucked my tail and scurried to the safe area beside Lee's desk and stayed there until long after the man moved down the hallway to the other rooms. Lee and Bella seem to think he's nice enough. I don't think people with pointy, bristly sticks know how to be nice. I don't know if it's their sticks that make them mean or if they are just born that way. But I do know I will never, ever trust anyone with that kind of stick. Ever.

Other than the grumpy man with the bristly stick and the fact that Lee and Tori don't take me to see Little Pup more often, I like our wake-yard-eat-school routine just the way it is. I know mostly what to expect.

Then, one day after school, Lee decides to add *dog class*.

"Want to go to class?" she says over and over as she grabs our bowls from the counter and prepares our evening meal.

Of course, Bella bounces around Lee's feet. Bella wants to do everything. I've met many dogs in my life—street dogs, family dogs, shelter dogs—but I've never met one with whiskers as white as Bella's that still wiggles and twists every time a human speaks in a high-pitched voice.

I don't wiggle or twist. I stand very still. My eyes dart from the safe spot under the kitchen table to the safe spot under the couch. Last winter, I would have raced for a hiding place at the sound of this new word, but more has changed than the weather. My body is fuller now. My coat is shinier, and I'm much less likely to scamper for safety than I was before Bella and Lee, which is why I follow them out to the car without even trying to run or hide on this cloudy evening.

When Lee's car stops in front of a tall brick building, the scent cloud of many, many dogs rushes inside my nose. The only time I've ever smelled this many dogs in one place was at the shelter, but those dogs smelled mostly scared and sick. These dogs smell healthy and energetic, like they're ready to hunt rabbits or chase squirrels.

Lee pushes her door open and steps out, then comes around to our side. "Okay, Bella. Let's show Millie how we do class."

As Lee leads us to the building, the first drops of rain spit from the sky. She shoves a small piece of metal inside a hole in the doorknob. When she pushes it open, bells jingle and clang. The door closes behind us, and thunder rumbles in the distance. The smell of many dogs grows stronger—big dogs, little dogs, fast dogs, slows dogs, every kind of dog I've ever met and more.

Lee taps a button on the wall, and light floods a huge room filled with children's playground equipment. We step onto a cushy, matted floor, and Lee waves her hand toward small fences and enormous plastic tubes at the other end of the large space.

"Bella, show Millie around while I set up," she says and steps toward a table covered with small stacks of papers.

Bella zooms across the room, disappears into one end of a tube, then shoots out the other end, head held high and prancing like a young horse.

"Go ahead, Millie. Have fun before the other dogs arrive." She swishes her hand toward Bella.

I've learned to pay close attention to Lee's hands. When I follow their direction, Lee usually gives me cheese. Tonight, the scent of many treats pours from the pouch she wears attached to her waist.

Whatever we're about to do involves lots and lots of human food, so I do what Lee wants and scurry toward Bella at the other end of the large room. Bella fake charges me like a puppy, then turns and runs the other way. I trot along behind her until she reenters the tube. I want to please her and Lee, but I don't want to be trapped in that confined space in this strange building, where I can't see what's going to happen next.

MILLIE

Suddenly, the bells on the door clang and jangle. My body tenses. My head swivels from Bella to Lee.

"Bella. Millie. Come," Lee commands.

Bella races to her, smacks her behind to the ground, and sits attentively at her feet. I peer in the direction of the clanging bells. I want to go to Lee, but I don't know who or what is coming through the door behind her. It could be the man with the bristly stick, for all I know.

"Millie! Come!" she commands in her top-dog voice and reaches inside the pouch strapped to her waist.

I don't know whether it's her voice or the cheese she's reaching for that pushes my paws into motion, but I trot forward.

"Good girl, Millie. Yes!" She pinches many bits of cheese from the stick in her pouch and feeds them to me and Bella.

As she slips a rope around my neck, a very heavy dog with a very smushed face huffs toward us, pulling a small, huffing man behind him.

Lee smiles at the man, then turns to Bella. "Bella, go to your place." She points to a raised dog bed in the middle of the room. Bella wags, crosses the room, then climbs into her spot and collapses with a *humph*.

When Lee turns back to the man, she extends her hand. "You must be Steve."

"Yes, and this is Bruno." He reaches down to pet the panting dog. They seem to be exerting too much energy breathing to really notice me.

"I got the shot records and the registration form you emailed, so you're all set." Lee smiles when she glances down to check on me, then turns back to the man. "You're a few minutes early. Why don't you walk Bruno around? Let him get comfortable with the building. Then pick one of the Klimb platforms to be your training spot for the evening. We'll get started when the others arrive."

"They're gonna get drenched if they don't get here soon," he mumbles as he and his dog head off to sniff around.

Lee loops my rope around her wrist, then turns to shuffle the papers on the table, and the bells jangle again. A woman and a tall, curved dog with the skinniest stick legs I've ever seen enter. Behind them are another dog and another human.

And behind them are Tori and a man who smells like Pops—all sweet like bread and hot brown liquid. But this man wears some kind of black plastic coat that crinkles when he moves and carries a dripping stick wrapped in the same crinkly cloth. I want to go to Tori, but I'm frozen. My slick pads won't move in the direction of that dripping stick.

"Millie!" Tori smiles and walks straight to me. "How are you, little girl?"

The man, shaking water from his coat, looks like Pops. He smells like Pops. But draped in that strange cloth, he does not move like Pops. And I don't like it.

Thankfully, he keeps his distance while I drink in the smell of Tori and wiggle beneath her warm hands. Lee is a wonderful human, but I always have to share her with Bella or with children at school or with David, who stopped by the house again last night.

But Tori only has eyes for me. It's like she sees me and nothing else when we're together. I've spent so much time hiding. I didn't know how good it could feel to be seen and known by a human.

But I like it. A lot.

MILLIE

When Tori sits on the matted floor and pulls me to her chest, I melt. She rubs her cheek to mine. I lick her face, and a wave of airy giggles escapes her lips and tickles my whiskers. Snuggling in her arms, with the ring of her laughter in my ear, feels natural. Almost like it's what I'm supposed to be doing. Like hunting for rats, chewing a bone, or looking out for Little Pup.

My head lifts when the doorbells jangle and ruin the moment. A rush of wet air invades the room. A crack of lightning breaks the sky outside the door. I can handle storms. I've survived enough on the streets, but my nose twitches at the scent of another human and dog entering the building. It's Jada and the old girl dog from the shelter.

My paws moisten with fear at the same time my tail swishes with joy. Jada is kind. I like her, but she also traps dogs in cages at the shelter. I don't know if I should wag or run. So I do nothing but lie perfectly still against Tori's chest.

And wait to see what will happen next.

Chapter Eighteen

Despite the thunder shaking the building and my confusion about Jada, what happens next is amazing. A tiny dog rushes through the door, then shakes a torrent of water from her white fur. She pulls an enormous man behind her, followed by a boy I barely recognize without a small, flat machine hiding his face.

It's Little Pup!

And her humans.

They're here.

At dog class.

I wiggle and wag.

"Good girl, Millie." Lee bends down and slips me a bit of cheese. "Good girl, Bella; stay," she calls across the room.

Bella lifts her head and thumps her tail but doesn't leave her raised bed. Even from far away, I smell her calm energy, and what's left of any fear or confusion about Pops, Jada, and the storm outside fades like a scent cloud on a windy day.

Lee wipes a drop of sweat from her face, slips my rope from her wrist, and hands it to Tori. "I need to talk to Jada real fast about an emergency with a dog at the shelter and get everyone checked in. Can you take Millie for me? Let her sniff around,

MILLIE

but don't get close to any dogs until I make sure everyone's up-to-date on their shots and that they're friendly, okay?"

"Okay." Tori nods and leads me away from Little Pup. I glance over my shoulder and flash what I hope is my best yellow-dog smile. Little Pup yips and bounces. I bounce a little, too, but it's no use. Tori leads me toward the tubes and playground equipment at the far end of the building.

Lee turns back to the man who smells like Pops but does not move like him. "Mack, you can sit here at the table or pull a chair to the training area if you'd like to stay and watch."

"Will do." The sort-of-Pops man unpeels himself from his black coat and sinks into the chair beside the table. When he drapes the strange cloth over the arm of the chair, it whispers, like it's almost alive.

Inhaling the perfume of all the dogs on the playground equipment, I watch as Lee heads to the group of people and dogs in the middle of the room. It seems like every healthy dog in the city has been here at some point—every healthy dog except Big Guy. There's still no hint of him anywhere.

When Lee claps her hands and interrupts my sniffing, Tori and I turn to watch.

"Tonight, we'll practice getting on and off the Klimb platforms. Good job to those of you who have already started." Her eyes narrow as she watches Little Pup squirming on her back on the floor. "They're a great way to keep the dogs focused. It helps them to have a defined work area. The most important dog training lesson you'll ever learn is the *watch me* command. Your dog can't learn anything if you don't have his undivided attention. Tonight, we're mostly going to practice *watch me* and walking on a loose leash. We'll work a little on *sit* too." Lee glances around the room.

I follow her eyes. A few dogs sit quietly beside their humans on small, raised tables. One dog stands on his table, smelling a little nervous. Little Pup jumps onto her table, squirms, falls off, and does it all over again. And again.

Lee talks on and on. "When you leave, I'll give you a printout of your homework and a preview of what we'll cover in the next few classes. Sound good?" She looks down at Bella, who smiles and takes it all in from her raised bed. "And in case you didn't know, this is my dog, Bella. She used to compete in all sorts of dog sports. She's retired now, but I use her to demonstrate the skills I teach in class."

The humans with the calm dogs nod and smile at Lee and Bella. The man and boy with Little Pup are too busy untangling themselves from her rope to look up.

"The little border terrier over there"—Lee points at me—"and the older girl over there"—she points at Jada and the girl dog from the shelter—"are rescues that will be available for adoption at Bark in the Park in a few weeks."

"I wish we could adopt you, Millie," Tori whispers in my ear as Lee drones on and on. "But Pops says I'm not even allowed to ask."

She sounds sad. So I wag for her, and it feels good. I'm used to working with other dogs, like Big Guy, and even helping other dogs, like Little Pup. Doing something to help a human is new, but I like how Tori giggles when I lick her face. When she giggles, her whole body relaxes. And when her body relaxes, mine grows and stretches in a whole new way—from the inside out.

"Tori," Lee calls from the center of the room, and we both turn to look. "Millie seems pretty comfortable. There's an open platform beside Skittles. Why don't y'all join us?"

"Want to try it, Millie?" Tori smiles down at me. When I swish my tail, she leads me toward the group.

Bella's tail thumps as we pass. Little Pup rolls onto her back on her table and whines. The huffing man with the huffing dog laughs. I would wag for Little Pup, except I know she needs to learn some manners. She won't make it in the human world or on the street with other dogs if she doesn't.

Lee speaks again and again. I did not think she could speak more words than she does at school, but somehow, she does. *Dog class* seems to require every human word in her language.

In between all the words, Lee invites Bella from her bed and has her move her body this way and that. Then Tori has me complete similar movements. I try very hard—not just for Tori but also because I want Little Pup to learn to behave from me the way I'm learning to behave from Bella. Tori gives me many treats when I look into her eyes, when I sit on my behind, and when I walk right beside her leg on the rope.

Over and over, Lee walks from one dog and human to another, saying more and more words while Tori and I practice looking at each other.

Finally, Lee returns to Bella and faces the whole group. "Good job, guys. That was an excellent class. I'm super impressed with how far everyone came in one night, even the little energetic ball of fluff." She waves her hand at Little Pup.

Several people laugh.

"At the end of the eight weeks, I'll offer the American Kennel Club Canine Good Citizen Test. It's a great first step toward therapy dog training or any other dog sports or activities you might want to try in the future."

I glance over at Little Pup. She's lying quietly on her table. All the sights, sounds, and activity seem to have finally worn her out. I wag for her, and she wags back without rolling off her table.

"One of the skills on the test is greeting a friendly stranger." Lee pauses and looks around the group. "We'll practice that on the way out." She smiles at the man who smells and looks like Pops. "Mack, would you be willing to be the friendly stranger?"

"Sure." The man stands and steps toward us. Without the crinkly black cloth billowing around his arms and legs, he's clearly Pops.

"Wait." Lee holds up a hand to stop him. "Why don't you put the raincoat back on. Hats, umbrellas, raincoats, canes, wheelchairs—those are all things we want to make sure our dogs are accustomed to, whether they go on to take the therapy dog test or not."

Pops shoulders rise and fall. "Sure," he says as he lifts the terrible black cloth from the side of his chair and drapes it over his body again.

I blink and blink. The man is practically a stranger again. When he steps toward us, the strange cloth swishes around his legs, disguising his movements. He looks sort of like a giant black bird with a human Pops head on top.

My body tenses. The huffing dog blinks like he also realizes something is not quite right. Bella lifts an ear. The tail of the old girl from the shelter stiffens, but other than that, the rest of the group barely seems to notice anything is wrong with the man or his clothes.

"You're okay, Millie," Tori soothes like she senses my uncertainty.

I do not wag. I swallow the growl building in my throat.

"Shhhh, Millie." Tori hands me several tiny bits of cheese, just like Lee, then rubs her hand along my back. "You're okay. You're okay," she repeats over and over.

But I'm not okay.

I'm horrified because I really need to *go potty*.

And if that man comes any closer, I'm going to *go potty* right here.

Right now.

In front of all these dogs and humans.

Chapter Nineteen

As the sort-of-Pops man steps toward the curved dog with the skinny stick legs, my body stiffens from the back of my head to the tip of my tail. My paws slip on the raised table.

"May I pet your dog?" The man's black cloth rustles around his legs when he leans toward the woman.

She nods. "Yes, please." A smile stretches from one side of her face to the other. Her dog blinks up at the man as he runs a hand along its neck, then moves to Jada and the dog from the shelter. The old girl is either too tired or too old to put up a fuss, even though I smell a puff of fear on her breath from way over here.

The huffing dog with the squished face seems to have a better sense of danger. He, at least, shrinks back a little when the Pops-man reaches for him. Little Pup, who has no sense of danger, jumps on the man's leg just like she does to everyone else. When her nails scratch the crinkly material, I jump to the ground.

"It's okay." The Pops-man leans to the side and looks at my face. His strange coat brushes the floor.

MILLIE

I cower behind Tori, trying to hide the tiny spot of wetness on my backside. My paws slip. I want to run, but I can't. I'm attached to Tori by the annoying rope.

"Mack, wait." Lee speaks low and slow, the way she sometimes speaks to children at school.

The Pops-man straightens and turns to look at her.

"She's afraid of the coat. I was a little worried about that. Just say *hello* to Tori, shake her hand, then walk away. We don't ever want to push a frightened dog."

The Pops-man shakes Tori's hand the way humans do when they first meet, which makes no sense if he's Pops because he and Tori know each other very well. I whine. My tail stiffens. Then he turns to go just as suddenly as he arrived. I exhale, thankful the wetness on my backside did not actually reach the floor.

"Thanks, Mack." Lee clasps her hands together near her chest. "This is a teachable moment. We have to know and respect our dogs' feelings. Forcing a fearful dog to confront the fear source can permanently break a dog's trust in us. Always give your dog an opportunity to retreat to a place where it feels safe. Then assess the situation and plan ways to gradually condition a positive response to whatever is causing the fear."

The tall lady with the funny dog nods. Jada tilts her head thoughtfully. The dog with the squished face plops onto the floor and closes his eyes like he's more exhausted by all the talking than I am. Thankfully, the man who looks and smells exactly like Pops has crinkled and swished his way back to his seat on the other side of the room.

"I've been working with Millie for a while," Lee continues. "She's become much less afraid of humans. But even dogs that love people can be put off by long coats, Halloween costumes, swishy dresses—anything that changes or hides the way we move."

The skinny lady with the skinny dog raises her hand.

"Go ahead." Lee nods encouragingly.

"I thought dogs had better eyesight than ours. Why are they confused by costumes and swishy clothes?" The woman's lips pucker, like she has a bad taste in her mouth.

"That's a common misconception." Lee smiles at the woman. "Their eyesight is actually pretty blurry—worse than ours in some ways, but they have way better night vision. And their eyes are ten or twenty times better at detecting movement than ours. From a distance, dogs recognize us by the way we move, the tilt of our shoulders, the length of our footsteps, and, of course, by our scent, not by the color of our hair or the shape of our faces."

"Who knew?" Little Pup's large man bends down to look in her eyes and kiss her on top of the head.

She licks his cheek. I'm happy she isn't falling off her table anymore and that I didn't wet the floor in front of her. I enjoy being here with Tori too. But I need to go back to Lee's house. I'm very tired and want Lee to quit talking and talking.

"So, we'll work on gradually introducing raincoats to Millie in a positive way."

My ears perk when she says my name. Maybe we can leave now.

"I'll probably place one on the floor in the kitchen where she eats. If she can handle that, I'll place it closer to her bowl. Then I'll drape it across a chair while I feed her treats."

We do not leave. Lee has too many words left to speak.

MILLIE

"Millie will gradually come to associate the sight and smell of the raincoat with something positive, like food. If at any time her fear increases, I'll go back and spend more time where she was comfortable. It may take a while, but I think she'll be okay. She's learning to trust me. I'll eventually work up to wearing the coat around her and then meeting strangers in a variety of coats. Does that make sense?"

Even Little Pup's humans nod now that she's mostly still and quiet on her raised table.

Lee smiles at the group. "Grab your homework on the way out. There's information on the back about Bark in the Park. Does anybody have any questions?" She glances around the room.

No one speaks. The humans smell as tired as their dogs. For once, they all seem to have run out of words. Only Little Pup springs to life when her humans release her from her table. She trots to me—head and tail held high—but she doesn't nip or head bump. Wagging, I lower my muzzle and let her lick the side of my mouth.

We rub faces like we did in the nest back when the days were short and cold. Exhaling, I clear my nostrils, then press my nose to her ear and inhale. Her healthy smell helps my insides relax.

"See you next week." Lee waves as humans grab papers from the table and lead their dogs out into the rainy night. She taps her thigh for Bella to follow, then walks toward me and Tori. "Didn't they do great?" She waves a hand at us and flashes her friendly teeth at the Pops-man, who looks more like himself seated in the chair at the table, even though he's still draped in the crinkly cloth.

"I thought Tori did as well as the adults." He pushes himself up from his chair, and I freeze.

Lee blinks one eye. "I think she did better than most of the adults. She's a natural."

"Can I do it again next week, Pops?" Tori rises on the front of her feet when she speaks.

"Actually, Mack . . ." Lee's voice drops. Her eyebrows squeeze together. "Could I ask you a question—privately—before you leave? Tori, you stay with Millie, okay?"

"Okay." Tori sits on the floor and pulls me to her lap. "You did great, Millie. You showed Skittles how to behave, didn't you?"

The Pops-man follows Lee to a row of empty dog crates lined against the side wall of the building.

When Tori lifts me to her chest, I forget about the horrible scrunching sound of his clothes and his odd movements and drink in the wonderful perfume of Tori's books and bread and everything that makes her Tori. Her chest is so warm, I can't worry about the nervous smells leaking from the back of Lee's knees or the pinched look on Pops's face.

"There's an emergency with a dog . . . shelter . . . if I don't take . . . Zeus . . ." Lee's words drop to nothing but air. ". . . put to sleep. Desperately need . . . Millie . . . until Bark in the Park."

Nervous smells escape from under Pops's swishy coat, too, but his voice is deeper and easier to hear. "Now's not a good time. I'm shorthanded at the bakery. We're due for an inspection. And honestly, I don't want her to get too attached. She can't handle the inevitable separation down the road."

MILLIE

"What if she's braver and stronger than you think? What if *she* wants this?" Lee sounds younger. Her words almost hold a hint of a whine.

If I didn't know her better, I would think she was begging. But Lee is a top-dog person; she does not beg.

"Our landlord requires a pet deposit." The Pops-man just sounds tired.

"The shelter would cover the cost of the pet deposit." Lee rests a hand on his arm until he meets her eyes.

"She's due to resume visits with her mom soon." He glances at Tori, and his shoulders relax. His eyes soften, like a mother dog's. He cares about Tori a lot. "But you're right. It might be good for her. Let me think about—" His words break off, like he's in pain or has a bone stuck in his throat, but humans do not eat bones.

Tori tilts her head, as interested in their words as I am. Leaning her body against the Pops-man's leg, Bella nuzzles her head beneath his hand.

"Is everything okay?" Tori calls to them.

Thankfully, she is a smart, kind girl and does not put me down on the floor.

"Yep." Lee smiles and claps her hands lightly. "You and Millie did so great that your pops and I need to discuss where you and Millie go from here."

The Pops-man squints his eyes at Lee.

"Really?" Tori's chest lifts beneath me when she speaks. "I'd love to train her or—"

The Pops-man smiles and raises a stiff hand. Lee chuckles. My tail swishes lightly, thankful the painful look is gone from the man's face.

I'm learning that people's emotions change quickly. One minute, they smell scared or sad and water drips from their eyes. The next, they smell light, and laughter bubbles from their throats.

Right now, I'm thankful their choppy words are gone. Thankful our little group smells healthy and safe. Thankful to have the warm arms of a girl to cuddle in.

I will always long for Big Guy and Mother, Brother, and Sister. Sometimes I might even miss wandering the streets late at night. But I also like this life with Bella and Lee, and now Tori, very much.

If I lost them, my insides would do more than tug with emptiness.

They would rip and tear.

Chapter Twenty

The next morning, we wake before the sun. As Bella and I race to the back door, Lee grabs a hat from the kitchen counter and slides it over her hair. Ready to mark all my favorite spots, I ignore her sudden interest in placing hats on her head. Last night, she wore one around the house, which she's never done before.

Right now, I must remind the squirrels and rabbits who the real boss is around here, so I zig and zag my way around the yard, marking every time I stop. It's too dark for Bella and Lee to play ball, so Bella does her business quickly and trots back to the door.

Inside, Lee turns her back on us and reaches in a cabinet for a large cup with a handle, then flicks a button on the machine that heats the strong, brown water she drinks every morning. Bella and I stick very close to her feet, trying to remind her the routine is wake, yard, eat, and we've already done wake and yard. So, now it's time to eat.

Lee yawns, leans back on the cabinets, then peers down at us with sleepy eyes. "If I feed you this early, you'll be starving by lunch."

Plopping down on my backside, I stare up at her and try to look pitiful. Bella is not so patient. She bounces around Lee's feet and bumps her hand again and again with her nose. Her tail swishes a long, crinkly cloth hanging from a chair at the table. It's the same cloth the Pops-man wore all over his body last night. Waiting to see if Lee will reach for our food bowls, I ignore the dark cloth and track her movements with my eyes.

My mouth waters. Bella's toenails tip-tap the wood floor, but Lee still doesn't reach for our bowls. So I whimper like a pup, and finally, she seems to get it.

"Silly Millie, you're such a baby." She huffs like she's irritated. But her eyes are smiling, and she's reaching for our bowls.

Our bowls!

"Today's gonna be a big day, ladies." She scoops food from the plastic container under the sink. "Millie, you're going to go stay with Tori, so Bella and I can work with a new dog that needs a lot more help than you."

My mouth waters when she dumps food into our bowls and places them on the wood floor. I inhale the kibble, then wait for Bella to finish. If you ask me, she could eat a little faster. When she finally finishes, she licks her lips, then turns to wag for Lee. Bella never leaves any crumbs in her bowl, but I always scurry over to check, just in case.

The only thing different about this day, other than waking very early, is that Lee carries my bowl, my favorite hard toys, and an extra dog crate to the car before she leads us out to the driveway.

At school, the routine also stays the same. I have learned when the children come and go and when Lee will take Bella and me outside to do our business. I've also learned that reading and books are very, very important to humans, even more to some of them than clean carpet.

Sometimes, Lee reads to the children. Sometimes, they read to each other. Sometimes, they sit alone and stare at their books like they're reading inside their heads. My favorite is when they read to each other because Bella and I get to take turns sitting and listening to them.

When Tori reads to others, nervous smells leak from her whole body, not just from under her arms and behind her knees, which is strange because she seems like a very brave girl and reading doesn't look scary. But when she reads to me, her words flow smoother and faster than usual. Her face lights up when this happens, and she doesn't leak the nervous smells either.

Today, the children read to each other, and when they read to each other, they sit wherever they want, even on the floor. And it's my turn to listen to Tori all by myself. She chooses the book with the dark-haired girl on the cover again. She's read some of the words to me so many times I've started to understand them. There is one part where she always leans down and whispers, "In spite of everything, I still believe that people are really good at heart."

When she leans down, I either lick her hand or rub my nose against her cheek. Today, I rub her cheek. Her mouth smiles for me, but her eyes sag.

"I really want that to be true, Millie. I want to believe that people are good at heart, even my mama."

I sit very still and stare into her eyes, trying to show her that I'm listening very hard, even if I don't exactly understand all the words.

"Pops says she loves me—that she's going to therapy and trying very hard to get better for me. But that she has a disease." She wipes a drop of water from the corner of her eye. "I believe him, but it's still hard to trust her. She did some really bad things before I went to live with Pops."

I smell Tori's sadness, but I do not have words to comfort her. No dogs do. Our mouths aren't shaped right. Our tongues are too long. But I have been watching Bella, and I've learned that there are other ways to communicate with humans. So I scoot closer, lean the weight of my body against Tori's leg, then continue listening very carefully to her words.

"You understand me. Don't you, Millie?" She rubs the side of my face.

Bella's muzzle is longer than mine and better for smiling. Mine is too short, but I lift the hair above my eyes and try really hard anyway.

I'm so focused on Tori's eyes that I don't hear or smell the man with the bristly stick until he enters the room with a tall bowl of flowers and makes a rumbly sound in his throat. The other children fall silent. A stillness hangs over the room like the stillness before a thunderstorm. My tummy tightens, reminding me it's time for Lee to take me and Bella outside.

Lee jumps up from the chair behind her desk, where she was shuffling papers. "Oh, hi, Mr. Crouse."

"For you." He shoves the very sweet-smelling flowers toward her face with one hand. With the other, he grips his bristly stick.

Lee takes the flowers, places them on her desk, and pulls a small, stiff paper from the blooms. Her breath catches. Excited smells leak from her hands, which is very confusing. I'm not

MILLIE

sure how flowers springing up all over outside or how that small, stiff paper is very exciting.

But several children whisper to one another behind their hands like they're excited too.

"Who are they from?" Tori asks.

Lee smiles down at the paper like she doesn't hear her.

"Ms. Berry?" Tori speaks louder this time.

"Oh." Lee glances up, then shakes her head. "They're from my friend David."

"He must really like you." The boy Eric nods like he knows a lot about flowers.

A squirrel-like chitter of laughter trickles from Lee's lips.

"The kid's right, Ms. Berry," Mr. Crouse says. "You've got yourself an admirer." His stick rests very close to the boy with the fluffy white hair sitting on the floor near Lee's desk. The boy eyes the stick warily.

"Friends, you need to keep reading." Lee's eyes narrow as she glances from the children to the strap on her wrist. "I mean it." She waves her hands at them, then meets Mr. Crouse's eyes again. "I was going to catch you when the children go to specials. I wanted to ask you about working the concession stand at Bark in the Park in a couple weeks."

He scratches the spiky gray hairs on his chin and frowns.

"It's a paying gig." Lee's eyebrows rise on her face. "I can tell you more about it if you come back after the bell."

He nods. When he turns to leave, his stick brushes past the fluffy-haired boy. Thankfully, the boy scoots out of the way to safety.

The boy with the night-black hair and the matching eyes leans over to Tori. "Mr. Crouse is serious about keeping the floors clean," he whispers, then closes his book with a thump.

Lee glances from the flowers to the strap on her arm. "Friends, go ahead and put your books away and tidy up your areas. The bell is going to ring in just a minute." She smiles, but the nervous, excited smells still leak from inside her hands and behind her knees.

Tori hugs me. "I'll be back at the end of the day, Millie," she says, then scurries to push a chair under a table and join the clump of children at the door.

"Bella, Millie, come." Lee points to the spot beside her desk, and I follow Bella across the room.

Then the bell clangs, and Tori disappears into the river of children in the hallway.

My nose twitches. It's not because of the crackers in the trash can beside Lee's desk, and it's not because I'm worried about Tori. I know she will come back. It's not even because of the bowl of too-sweet flowers on Lee's desk. It's because of the sharp-chemical smell of the man with the bristly stick still lurking outside the classroom door.

Chapter Twenty-One

That day after school, Lee does not drive me and Bella back through the mountain to her house. She drives me to something called an *apartment building*, where we climb many stairs and walk down a carpeted hallway with many doors that smell like people of every shape and size and age and all the delicious foods they eat.

When Lee knocks on a door that smells like books and sweet bread and a young girl and an old man, I yip with joy.

"You're here," Tori yips with joy, too, when she swings the door open to let us in. Everything inside smells like Tori—the chairs, the carpets, even the walls—and when the wind blows through the open window, I smell the sweet-bread place nearby and a faint whiff of Little Pup.

"We're here with a special delivery," Lee says and sweeps her hand toward me. "And we brought everything you'll need to take care of her until Bark in the Park." She offers my rope to Tori. "I just need to get the dog food from the car. She's microchipped, of course, but I'd leave her collar on as often as possible just in case. You never know what can happen, especially in the city."

Bella prances to Pops and offers her head for petting. I stand on my back legs, bouncing and tapping Tori with my front paws, encouraging her to pick me up, which she does because she's the best girl ever.

"I can grab her food. I need to check the mail anyway." Pops reaches for the bag Lee carries that smells like my bowl and hard toys and sets it on a small table beside the door.

"Bella and I will go with you. Tori can show Millie around the apartment."

"Yes, I can." Tori turns away from Pops and Lee. "I'll show her my room first."

Pops and Lee talk and talk and talk as they lead Bella out of the apartment. The door clicks shut behind them, and Tori takes me to a room that must be where she sleeps. The bed smells so much like her if I close my eyes, it's hard to tell where her body ends and the bed begins.

She sits me on the softest blankets ever, then lies down so we can stare into each other's eyes. Sleeping in the bed with Bella and Lee is nice, but lying here is even better. In fact, it's so amazing, I don't even mind it when Bella and Lee leave me and my bowl and rope here.

My time at their house helped me understand human routines so well that I pick up on the Pops-Tori-apartment routine in just a few days. I do miss going to school with Lee and Bella, but it's okay because I get to rest, wrapped in Tori's scent, all day long and sleep in her bed at night. Under the covers! And I don't have to share her with any other dogs. She is all mine, and I am all hers.

Some days, she does not go to school at all, like today. Today is a Millie-and-Tori day. It is also an eggs-and-bacon day.

My mouth waters as Tori slides her feet into fuzzy shoes, and I follow her to the kitchen.

"Morning, sunshines! Hope you're hungry." Mrs. Smith, the lady from next door, smiles and waves a wooden spoon in the air. She arrives most days before the sun so Pops can work on his bread.

"Millie's always hungry." Tori yawns and grabs my rope from a hook on the wall.

"Hurry, then, before your eggs get cold." She points at Tori with her spoon.

I don't shy away or duck behind Tori's legs when she waves her spoon, like I would have when I lived on the street. I'm learning to feel safe with Tori and Pops and Lee and learning that humans point with their fingers and all sorts of other things and that pointing isn't necessarily a bad or scary thing.

Yesterday, Pops brought me a new bone—the largest, tastiest bone I've ever had that did not come from a trash can. Excited, I attacked it like I would a rat—biting it and shaking it one way and then the other. It scraped the sensitive skin above my teeth. Blood warmed my tongue. I sealed my lips and tried very hard not to dirty the carpet, but I was too slow. A dark streak stained the rug between my paws.

Abandoning the bone, I crept behind the couch. My insides tightened as I lowered my head and waited for Pops's loud words or Tori's waving arms, but there were no loud words or waving arms. Pops simply poured water on the stain, wiped it with a cloth, and took me and Tori for a walk, like nothing had even happened—like I hadn't even dirtied their precious carpet.

Now Tori slips my rope over my head and sneaks a piece of bacon from Mrs. Smith's plate. Licking my lips, I follow Tori and her piece of bacon out the door, down a long hallway, and down the stairs.

"Hurry, Millie, and I'll share my bacon." She pushes open a heavy door and leads me to the row of trees along the sidewalk out front. "Go potty," she says, pointing at the closest tree.

When I pull on the rope, Tori follows like a good girl. Her fuzzy shoes scuffle the sidewalk. The trees farther down the street are best. That's where Little Pup does her business. My tail wags my body when I smell her recent mark. She had bacon today too.

As I squat to leave Little Pup a message of my own, I hear the trash truck beep, beep, beep in the distance. Glancing up and down the street, I notice the cans lining the sidewalk and realize my belly has been so full of dog food and bits of meat and cheese for so long, I've almost forgotten what it feels like to be hungry—to have to hunt for food on trash day.

"Good girl, Millie. Yes." Tori offers me a glorious bit of her bacon.

Turning away from the overflowing cans, I gobble the delicious treat and follow Tori toward the apartment. Back inside, she places my morning meal on the floor and shares another bit of her bacon with me while Mrs. Smith bangs pans in the sink.

"Your Pops said Ms. Berry will be here for you in a little bit. He also said to remind you he needs your help cleaning the bakery this afternoon." Mrs. Smith wipes her wrinkled hands on a cloth, then joins us at the table.

"Got it." Tori gulps her fruity drink, then pushes back from the table. "Thanks for breakfast, Mrs. Smith."

"Of course." She takes Tori's plate, then steps back to the sink. "Your Pops has helped me more than you'll ever know.

Now, go brush your teeth and get dressed. Ms. Berry will be here any minute."

In the tiny room where the humans do their business, Tori scrapes her teeth with a tiny bristly stick. After she spits a sharp-smelling goo from her mouth, I follow her to her room and lie on the floor to rest my full belly. My eyes grow heavy as she changes from her sleeping clothes to her going-outside clothes, then grabs a hat from a small table beside her bed and slips it on her head. I would rather her tangles of curls hang loose down her back. Her Tori scent flows more freely that way, but even with the hat, she still smells like Tori. Her face still moves the same, so I ignore the hat the best I can.

When someone knocks on the door to the apartment, I dart to my feet, bark, and trot down the hall behind Tori. Even before she opens the door, the familiar scent cloud of dried sticks, many children, and many dogs leaks inside. My body wiggles and squirms like Little Pup's. I know that smell! It's Lee and Bella.

"Hi, little girl," Lee says as she slides an armful of books onto a table beside the door, then bends down and scoops me into her arms. She's wearing a hat, too, but I'm so excited to see her, I do not care. I woof joyfully, then lick her chin and face until she tilts her head back and laughs.

"I'm happy to see you too."

Bella stands at her side, wagging and smiling for me.

"Did someone switch dogs on me? This cannot be the dog I rescued from the pound just a couple months ago."

"It's her." Tori's chest puffs like it does when she reads to me.

When Lee sets me on the ground, I spring toward Bella. She bows her head playfully, then circles around to my backside. We circle and sniff, circle and sniff, circle and sniff. She ate chicken recently, and another dog's scent clings to her fur too—a large, young, boy dog.

"Did you bring Zeus?" Tori steps out of our way when Bella's tail swipes her leg.

"Not today. We're gonna practice for the CGC test. He's not ready for that." Her shoulders sag.

I wag for her and rub my side against her leg. Today is a wonderful day. We had eggs and bacon. We are all together. Her shoulders should not be sagging. We should be happy. Happy. Happy.

Lee stares past Tori like she forgot all about me and Tori.

"You'll help him, Ms. Berry. You taught Millie to trust humans." Tori's small body stretches to its full height. "And . . . you taught me how to read."

Lee blinks. Her eyes clear, like she remembers Tori and I are right here, ready to play and share the treats in her pockets. "I appreciate your confidence, Tori. I really do, but every rescue doesn't go as well as Millie's seems to be going. Sometimes, there are setbacks. Something unexpected can trigger an almost forgotten fear, and a dog can relapse suddenly. There are instances where no matter how hard you try, a dog just doesn't work out.' "

"That won't happen with Millie or Zeus." Tori speaks in a confident, top-dog voice.

Lee softly claps her hands. "Enough chitter-chatter. Grab a sweatshirt. We've got work to do."

Tori scurries off to her room and returns with another piece of clothing, then we head out of the apartment.

Together.

Like one big, healthy pack.

MILLIE

"Good girl, Millie." Tori pulls a piece of bacon from her pocket that I had completely forgotten about on our sniff-anything-you-want walk.

I thump my tail. Sometimes, I have to work for treats by sitting or spinning and twisting my body various ways. But I've also learned that Tori will give treats when I do nothing but sit quietly, especially if I sit quietly when there are new people or dogs around.

So I let out a breath from deep in my body and rest my head on my paws. A gentle breeze rustles the leaves above us. I twitch my ear when a pesky fly lands on it. It flies above my head, then lands on my other ear. I shake my head until my ears flap and snap against my face. When the fly lands on my nose, I snap my teeth at it.

Distracted by the rustling leaves and the bothersome fly, I don't smell the large boy dog until he's very close. When his scent presses inside my nose, I spring to my paws like Little Pup. My tail waves like a flag. I'd recognize the dark dog with white patches on his sides anywhere.

It's Big Guy!

On a rope.

Coming this way.

Right now.

Chapter Twenty-Three

A howl rises from deep in my chest as I spin around Tori's feet. It's Big Guy! He smells me, too, because his tail wags and wags—so hard it might fly off his body—and he's dragging a strange woman behind him. She has feet because they stick out from below her swishy clothes. She has hands because one of them holds Big Guy's rope. She might have a face, but all I see is a mouth. The rest of her face, if she has one, hides beneath the widest, floppiest hat and the largest dark circles I've ever seen.

Lee and Tori like it when I stand calmly and greet people face-to-face, but I can't this time. This woman is too different, so I slink partway between Tori's legs. My pads moisten on the cool pavement. Even Bella stands still and watches instead of wiggling and smiling.

"Hello." The woman lifts one hand, and tiny strings of bells jingle at her wrists. The swishy cloth she wears slides back, revealing an arm. Long strings of tiny balls click and clack around the woman's neck. "Can our dogs say hello?"

No nervous smells leak from behind Tori's or Lee's knees.

"Sure. Thanks for asking first." Lee steps toward the woman.

When she does, Bella flaps her tail and follows like she's decided the strange woman is okay after all. I'm not so sure. Inhaling, I twitch my nose one way, then the other, and sniff for any sign of danger, but the woman just smells like piles and piles of flowers, so I step forward to greet the strongest, bravest dog I've ever known.

Big Guy!

He lifts his ears in Bella's direction, but he has eyes only for me.

"This is Millie." Tori smiles as Big Guy nuzzles my ear. "She's a rescue."

I lick Big Guy's lips and inhale all of him while the humans talk. He smells different—like the inside of a house and dog food and this flowery woman. He hasn't eaten trash or lived on the street in ages. But he still smells fast and healthy.

"So is Lucky." The woman peels the dark circles off her face and hangs them from the string of clicking balls around her neck, then rubs her hand along Big Guy's side, and he lets her.

He is a very different Big Guy, and the woman actually has kind eyes now that I can see them.

"Is he the lucky one, or are you?" Lee scratches Bella behind the ears as she watches me and Big Guy.

I sniff Big Guy's backside, then plop on the sidewalk and roll on my back so he can smell the bacon I ate this morning and the apartment and even Little Pup, whom he never got to meet.

"Oh, he's the lucky one." The wind picks up, and her strange clothes rustle like the leaves above our heads.

But I stay stretched on my side and thump my tail for Big Guy.

MILLIE

"My husband hit him with his car during the blizzard last winter—broke two of his legs. Lucky had internal injuries. The vet said he wouldn't make it. But here he is." She pats his side again.

Bella can't stand it any longer. She steps forward to sniff and be sniffed. Big Guy licks the side of her mouth in respect for her age. I stand to join them—not wanting to be left out.

"He wasn't microchipped. No one claimed him, so we nursed him back to health." Now the woman scratches him right above his tail. "We love him."

Big Guy looks up at the woman and flashes his best yellow-dog smile, but he is not a yellow dog. He is a street dog—the toughest street dog I've ever known. He never used to like humans. But something has changed because he stares at this woman the way Bella stares at Lee.

"You hear such bad things about pit bulls, but I swear he's a marshmallow." The woman rubs his ear like she can't keep her hands off him.

"I've known some good ones. It's like anything else. You have to get to know the individual dog. You can miss out on a forever friend if you choose them based purely on the way they look."

"Totally agree." Something beeps inside the woman's swishy clothing, and she pulls out one of the small, flat machines that humans love to stare at and talk to. "Precious dogs. Gotta get this." She waves the machine at Lee and Tori, then tugs on Big Guy's rope. "Come on, Lucky," she says in the high-pitched voice humans usually use on puppies.

He wags for me and rubs his cheek against my cheek like he's telling me it will be okay or he'll be back. I'm not sure which. Then he turns and follows the woman.

I whine and wag, begging him to stay.

His tail droops. He looks from the woman to me and back to the woman. When he follows her, he doesn't look back again.

My insides tug and twist like he's taking a part of me with him. I whimper.

"Millie, what's wrong? You did so well, little girl." She lifts me to her chest and makes funny noises when she squishes her lips to the top of my head. "Didn't she do great, Ms. Berry, with the woman's hat and glasses and all that?"

Lee reaches over and scratches me behind the ears. She squishes her lips to the top of my head, too, like I'm a human baby. But Lee is a top-dog person, and she never treats dogs like human babies.

My body melts like snow beneath her squishy lips. I don't want Big Guy to go. I hope to see him again and again, like Little Pup. But even if I don't, I can tell by the smells he shared with that woman that she is his pack now, the same way Tori is mine.

Chapter Twenty-Four

"We're home," Tori says as she shoves the door to the apartment open and bends down to slip the rope off my neck.

When we enter, silence hangs in the front room. I smell Pops and his sweet bread before I see him sitting slumped at the kitchen table in the dark.

"Where's Ms. Berry?" He smiles, but his face looks brittle, like a dried leaf, when he pushes his chair back from the table and stands to greet Tori.

"She had stuff to pick up for Bark in the Park." Tori tosses my rope into the bowl on the little table just inside the door, then heads toward the kitchen.

"Her order for the concession stand is about enough to do me in. I've been baking dog biscuits in between regular orders for days. Thankfully, hers can be done ahead." Pops shakes his head, runs a hand through his thin hair, then smiles down at me when I nose-bump his leg to try to remind him to greet me too. "Hey, little girl. How'd you do at the park?"

"She met a lady in a long flowy dress and a weird hat and did great. And watch this." Tori's hand disappears inside the pocket where she keeps my treats.

I swivel around to face her, wiggling my body like Bella to show her I'm ready for a treat.

"Millie, sit." She lifts a tiny ball of cheese to the middle of her chest.

Lifting my eyes to hers, like we've been practicing, I rock back on my behind and wait for the cheese that I know will be mine.

"Stay." She holds up a stiff hand.

My ears twitch. She sounds very serious, so I don't move.

"Good girl, Millie. Yes!" She gives me the cheese, then turns to Pops. "So now I just keep waiting a tiny bit longer each time to give her the treat, and she eventually connects the word *stay* and being still with getting a treat."

When Pops waves his knotty hand from me to Tori, the lines between his eyes relax. "You're really good at this, Tori."

"I know." Her eyes shine when she flashes her teeth at him.

Then the small mechanical box Pops talks into buzzes on the table. When he turns it over, his eyes pinch together again. "It's your mom."

"Oh." The light in Tori's eyes flickers.

"You want to answer it?" Pops nudges the vibrating box across the table.

Tori's teeth press into her lip like she's biting herself, then nods. "Sure." Nervous chemicals twinge the air, seeping from her mouth. She seems worried about the box all of a sudden, which doesn't make any sense.

I've seen her speak words into it many times. Nose-bumping her leg and wagging my tail, I try to remind her it's a Tori-and-Millie day and that she should be joyful, but she doesn't seem to see me, which is also very strange. She always sees me.

She lifts the box and swipes it with her thumb. "Hi, Mom." Her voice rises and falls, making her sound younger than she normally sounds.

The muffled words of another human hum inside the box.

"I'm good. How are you?" Tori's words even out the longer she speaks. "Pops is right here. I'll put you on speaker."

Pops grips his hands on the table in front of him. The side of his face twitches as Tori pulls the box away from her ear, then presses it with her finger. "You there?" Tori asks.

"I'm here." A woman's voice blares from the box like she's inside the room with us. "Have y'all had a good week?"

"We have." Pops unclasps his hands and wipes them on his pants under the table.

"We really have. Remember Millie, the dog I told you about? I taught her *down*. We're working on *stay*." Tori places the box on the table and slips into a chair beside Pops. "Millie likes it when I read to her, and I wrote a poem about her."

My tail flutters. The more Tori speaks my name, the more her body relaxes. The nervous smell on her breath fades away. Tired from all the sniffing at the park and the excitement of finding Big Guy, I plop to the floor under the table and rest my head on her foot.

The humans drone on and on. The cool floor feels nice on my warm belly. Tori and Pops seem less worried, so I close my eyes. When the woman's voice drops, I lift an ear and open my eyes.

"I'm . . . allowed . . . to have"—the woman's words break and chop in odd places—"visitors next weekend. My therapist says I've made lots of progress. I've been clean for over thirty days now." Her words pick up speed until they almost run together.

Tori's toes clench beneath my head. Sensing she might want to rest her hand on my head, I scurry to stand beside her chair. She can't see me because her eyes are locked on Pops's face.

"Rachel, let me talk to Tori about it, okay?" He grabs the box, touches it with his finger, then presses it to his ear. "Next weekend is Bark in the Park. We've had it planned for weeks."

The woman's words fade and hum inside the box again.

"Right." Pops nods. When he glances at Tori, the corners of his lips lift but remain tight and thin. "Right."

He repeats the word *right* several times, like he's forgotten how to say any other words.

"Right," he says again. "I'll let you two say goodbye. You and I can talk more later tonight or tomorrow. Okay?"

He brushes his finger against the phone, and the woman's voice roars out again.

"Okay. I love you, Tori. I'm proud of all your hard work at school and with Millie."

Tori's back straightens. She looks like herself again—more young human and less helpless puppy. "Thanks, Mom. I love you too. Bye."

"Bye." The woman's voice cracks like she has a piece of food caught in her throat.

Pops gently touches his finger to the box, then lowers it to the table. He and Tori stare at each other like two different forest creatures seeing each other for the first time.

"Well . . ." Pops breathes long and slow from his mouth. "That's a lot to think about, isn't it?"

"Yes." Tori twists my ear between her fingers.

I sit very still, not wanting her to stop. Thankfully, she bends over and lifts me to her chest so I can nuzzle my face in the curls falling around her shoulders. Pops sits frozen in place, like a rock in the alley out back.

Tori runs her hand along my back. "She sounds better—almost like she sounded before she hurt her back and started taking all that medicine."

I flatten my body against her chest the way Tori likes.

"And you always say people can change."

"They can. Just like dogs." Pops reaches over and runs his hand along my back too. "They have to want to, though, and change is hard. Sometimes it doesn't work the first time or the second or the twenty-second, for that matter. But it's always possible."

Tori rubs the side of her face against the side of mine. "Look at Millie."

"Yes." Pops tussles my ears and laughs. "Look at Millie. She's the perfect example of change—street urchin turned love muffin. If she can change and grow and learn to trust, we all can."

"Ms. Berry and dog class made a difference for Millie." Tori's eyes light up like Pops is going to give her a cookie or something even better. "I think maybe all the classes and group sessions at the residential facility are making a difference for Mom too."

Finally, they're both smiling again, which means we can forget about the voice in the talking box and get back to enjoying the rest of this Tori-and-Millie-and-bacon-and-eggs day.

Chapter Twenty-Five

The next day, a dark sky drops rivers of water on our building. Tori and I leave the apartment only to dart to the tree right outside the door. Ignoring the crinkly cloth Tori drapes all over her body, I squat quickly. When we race back inside, I shake water from my fur. Tori peels the crinkly cloth from her body, and everything underneath it is dry. The strange cloth is actually quite amazing—better even than my wiry outer coat for keeping things dry underneath. I still do not like the way it tricks my eyes and disguises human movements, but I now understand why humans like it so much.

Back inside, Pops pats the couch for us to join him. "My all-time favorite dog movie is on." He points to the box that hangs on the wall that humans love to watch. "Dry Millie off and join me."

"Okay." Tori grabs a cloth from the table where she tossed my rope and rubs me down with it, which feels wonderful. Then she folds the cloth in chunks, places it back on the table, and joins Pops on the couch.

Claiming the spot between them, I rest my head on Tori's leg and press my backside against Pops. When I was a street dog, I had to choose between eating or staying dry. When I could, I chose to stay dry, but being comfortable on the outside made the hunger on the inside almost unbearable. Now I don't have to choose. I can have both.

"It's not sad, is it?" Tori asks as she scratches the good spot between my ears.

Pops rests his warm hand on my side, near my full belly, and I sink further into the soft couch. "I might have shed a tear or two, but it's also funny and heartwarming. And a great story about how important it is for everyone to have at least one good friend. For Willie, the boy in this movie, that one true friend happens to be a scrappy little terrier named Skip."

Tori's fingers freeze. She sits so still I can't tell if she's taking air into her body.

I whine for her, trying to remind her to breathe.

She stares at Pops's hand on my side. "Pops, I know I promised I wouldn't ask"—her words rustle like the flap of a baby bird's wings—"but can we please—"

"Tori, no." Pops's hand stiffens. Deep lines threaten to crack his face into pieces.

Twisting my head, I lick his hand, wanting him to relax and watch the box on the wall. My ears droop when he does not.

"We just . . . I'm afraid—" Scared, nervous chemicals leak from his hands when he turns to face her.

She squeezes her hands together near her face. "Please. You always say when we're afraid of someone or something, it usually means we should lean in and learn more about them and their lives."

He levels his eyes on her. Now he's frozen in place, too, his jaw clamped tight. They're like two dogs sizing each other up.

"I was talking about meeting new people with different political and religious beliefs from us. You know that."

Tori does not look away. She plants her hands on her hips, making herself look larger than she really is. "Well, I have a different belief about keeping Millie than you do."

Pops glances down at me. He exhales. When he lifts his eyes again, the skin beneath them droops lower than my ears. He suddenly looks very tired. "Tori, I promise, when the time is right, when you're a little older and we know more about the situation with your mom, we will get a dog."

"I don't want *any* dog." Tori's hands twist into balls. Her foot taps the floor. "I want Millie."

Pops rubs his face. "I don't have any help at the bakery. I'm due for an inspection. I just . . . I can't do this right now." His body shrinks in on itself, making him look much smaller than usual.

"If we don't do something right now, someone's going to adopt Millie at Bark in the Park, and I'm never going to see her again." Tori stands and scampers toward her room.

My head twists from Tori's stiff back to Pops's creased face and back to Tori. Standing, I whine for Pops, trying to tell him I'm sorry that I cannot stay on the couch with him.

"I'll be okay, Millie. Go with her." He turns his lips into something like a smile, then presses a button to silence the box on the wall.

Tucking my tail between my legs, I hurry to Tori's room. She's curled in a ball on her bed with her legs pulled to her belly. Water streams from her eyes. Dark blotches dot her face, but she does not smell sick. She smells sad, which doesn't make any sense. We were just cuddling on the couch together.

MILLIE

Now, all of a sudden, Pops looks like he's hurt, and Tori squeezes her eyes shut and gasps when she breathes. I jump onto the bed to lick her face. She unbends her legs and makes room for me to curl into her side.

"I shouldn't have been mean to him." She rubs her nose and swipes at her eyes when she talks. "He has a lot of stress. I love him. He takes care of me. He tried to take care of Mom, even after she took money from the bakery . . ."

She rubs slow circles on my ear. When her eyes close, her breathing quiets.

My chest rises and falls with Tori's, like it does at night when she's asleep. Not wanting to wake her, I lie very still, like I did in the nest with Little Pup. Even when Pops's footsteps shuffle up the hall toward us, I remain frozen like a lamppost on the street.

He pauses in the doorway to Tori's room. When his eyes land on her sleeping face, they soften. "I have to head back to the bakery. Mrs. Smith is on her way over." He pauses to look at my face as if he's talking to another human. "You really are a good girl, Millie. I wish things were different."

Lifting the fur above my ears, I try very hard to pull the corners of my lips into a yellow-dog smile and tell him not to worry—that as long as I'm with Tori, everything will be okay. I will take good care of her just like I took good care of Little Pup and just like Big Guy took care of me.

But he doesn't seem to understand. When he heads down the hall and away from us, his eyes and shoulders sag. Sadness leaks from under his arms, behind his knees, the inside of his hands, even the backs of his ears.

My insides tighten.

A whimper catches in the back of my throat.
Something is terribly wrong.
But what?

Chapter Twenty-Six

Lying perfectly still, I curl against Tori's tummy, wondering how a day that started with warm blankets and books cracked and crumbled into Tori's blotched face and Pops's sagging shoulders. Then Mrs. Smith shuffles back into the apartment. I prick my ears to listen but don't leave Tori's side.

My nose twitches at the wonderful aroma of the cooked meat Mrs. Smith brought into the apartment with her. I try very hard but cannot contain the squirm that starts at my tail and travels up my body.

Opening her eyes, Tori stretches her arms above her head. "I didn't mean to fall asleep." She ruffles my ears, slings her legs over the side of the bed, and slides her feet into the strappy shoes she kicked off before flinging herself down earlier.

"Glad you're alive," Mrs. Smith calls in her twittery bird voice from the kitchen.

"Mm-hmm." Tori swipes her curls away from her face.

I hop to the floor and follow her down the hall. My mouth makes water as we head toward the yummy smells in the kitchen.

Mrs. Smith stands over the hot box in the kitchen, stirring something with a wooden spoon.

"Are you hungry?" she asks without turning to look at us.

"No." Tori plops down at the kitchen table and rests her head in her hands.

Resting my head on her warm foot, where I can breathe in all her wonderful smells, I plop down too.

Mrs. Smith wipes her hands on the cloth tied around her neck and turns to face us. "Why so glum?"

"Pops and I argued about Millie." Tori's face sinks closer to the table, like it's too heavy for her hands.

"Oh?" Mrs. Smith's eyebrows rise toward her white hair. "He's under a lot of pressure right now. I bet it will all work out."

"I don't. Millie will get adopted at Bark in the Park, and I'll never see her again."

I brush my tail back and forth on the floor at the sound of my name, hoping Tori's mood will improve.

"Oh, sweetie." Mrs. Smith steps over to Tori and rests a squishy hand on her shoulder. "Would a snickerdoodle cupcake make you feel better?"

"Probably not." Tori's words sound short and tight, but her head does lift a little.

"Why don't we just try?" Mrs. Smith turns away and opens the cold box where Pops and Tori store food, then pulls out a ball-like mound of what smells like the sweetest bread ever. "Your pops isn't the only one who can bake around here." Her eyes sparkle with tiny bits of light when she places the bread ball in front of Tori.

MILLIE

Tori swipes her finger across the sticky goo on top, then licks her finger. The side of her mouth rises a bit higher. "Mmmm. That *is* good."

Nose-bumping her leg, I try to remind her that I'm right here. I stayed with her when water streamed from her eyes. I would stay with her no matter what—even if she chose not to share her bread ball, although I really, really hope she decides to share it.

Despite the fact that she's a child, she is one of the best dog people ever because she pokes the goo on top again and bends down to offer me her finger.

I lick quickly before she changes her mind. My tail swipes the floor, back and forth, back and forth, over and over, and Tori smiles for the first time since her face-off with Pops.

"That's my girl." Mrs. Smith rubs Tori's back, then returns to the meat sizzling on the hot box. "When you finish, you should go help your pops at the bakery. He's been so shorthanded, and the health inspector was at the sandwich place around the corner yesterday. They'll probably be at the bakery in the next day or two."

Tori swallows another large bite of the fluffy bread and rich goo, then licks her lips. "Okay. Will you stay here with Millie?" Like the best girl ever, she bends down and extends the last bit of her treat to me. But the spark in her eye disappears with the last of the yummy goodness, and the sad chemical smell seeps from behind her knees again.

"Yep. I'll grab my book from next door. Then Millie and I can sit and read until the stew finishes."

Before I know what's happening, Tori bends down, squeezes me in her arms, then turns to leave.

My tail hangs between my legs as I follow her to the door.

"She won't be gone long, Millie Vanillie." Mrs. Smith tugs on the thin string tied around her neck, pulls the white cloth covering her clothes away from her body, and drapes it across the back of the couch.

I paw at the door.

"Let me grab my book. Then we can rest until Tori comes back." She opens the door just wide enough for her body to squeeze through, then gently pulls the door closed.

I sit back on my haunches to wait. I know Tori, Pops, and Mrs. Smith will not leave me alone for too long. Bella taught me to wait patiently for humans to return—not to scratch at doors, dig in couches, or chew things like baskets.

But my paws moisten anyway. Today feels different, and I can't help myself. I inspect the door with my nose, then scratch it and scratch it again.

And it creaks open.

The door is open! There is no rope around my neck. The hall is empty. My humans are gone. So I poke my head outside the door and sniff one way and then the other. Humans, even good ones like Lee and Tori, do not like it when dogs rush out of open doors and gates without them.

But I'm not running away or rushing out alone.

I'm doing something good.

I'm going to find my girl.

Chapter Twenty-Seven

Stepping carefully into the hallway, I lower my head to the carpet and sniff for Tori. My nose leads me past the apartment that smells like Mrs. Smith and down the stairs to the room with many small metal boxes hanging on the wall.

The glass door that opens to the street is closed tight. I bump it with my nose and scratch it forcefully with my front paws, but it does not budge. Panting, I sit back to catch my breath and prepare myself to start digging. But I do not have to dig because something amazing happens. A man loaded down with packages approaches the door, shoves it open with his foot, and staggers inside.

My street-dog instincts take over, and I slip out the door and onto the sidewalk, completely unnoticed by human eyes. Outside, I must choose whether to follow my nose toward the park, Little Pup and the human she lives with, or Tori, Pops, and their bread. Or I could choose a completely different path. I could follow my nose back to street life, to a new alley, and to a life without fences, doors, and ropes.

A breeze rustles the trees that line the sidewalk and pushes a dark cloud in front of the sun that tried to peek out while Tori was napping. The smell of Pops's sweet bread tickles my nose. My insides squeeze, but it's not hunger tugging at my sides. And it's not the old, empty feeling that's a constant part of life on the street. It's a tugging for the people who make me feel full inside and out—Tori and Pops.

Lifting my nose to the sweet smell of bread, I trot along the sidewalk toward the entrance to the alley. Wet pavement chills my pads. The stink of rats pricks my nose. A large piece of wood blocks the opening to the nest I shared with Little Pup.

I don't care. I'm not here to fight rats or sleep in the nest. I'm here to find my girl, which is why I hurry to the back door of the bakery and scratch and scratch and scratch. When no one comes to let me in, I press my nose to the door.

Tori's and Pops's fresh scent clouds slip through the crack around the door along with the smell of two adult men I do not recognize. And Tori and Pops smell very nervous. Standing on my back legs, I scratch and scrape the door—harder this time—like I'm tunneling for a rat. When that doesn't work, I bark. And bark. And bark.

Tori's scent cloud rushes through the cracks around the door. She opens it a little and peeks out. My tail waves like the flag in the park. I bounce and wiggle like Little Pup, showing her that I am here. I found her. She and Pops do not need to worry.

But when I push my head through the cracked door and try to squirm inside, something horrible happens. Tori shuts the door on my body. Shocked by the pressure on my sides, I squeal like a wounded pup.

MILLIE

Tori sucks in air. Her eyes widen with pain, like she's the one being squeezed. She opens the door a little, and when she does, I see the horrible bristly stick gripped in her hands.

"What is that?" A strange man holding a thin board with papers attached to it stands with Pops inside the back of the bread place.

"It's nothing. Just the wind," Tori calls over her shoulder to the man inside. "Millie, go. You can't be here. You'll ruin the inspection," she hisses.

I freeze. I do not recognize this girl with the angry, panicked face. The evil stick has done something horrible to Tori. Fearing it will do something worse to me, like poke my paws or shoot hot rocks at my backside, I clamp my tail between my legs and hang my head. My jaws tighten. My insides clench and tug. And not with hunger or even the empty feeling of street life. This tugging is like being rolled on my back by a coyote and having my insides ripped out.

"You have to go," she spits and brushes me out the door with her bristly stick.

So I run.

And run.

And I keep running, even when Tori steps into the alley behind me and cries my name like she's the one having her insides ripped out instead of me.

Chapter Twenty-Eight

My paws bite at the sidewalk. My tongue hangs from the side of my mouth. I dart past a woman carrying a baby and dodge a man who squats and tries to speak to me. My sides heave, but I do not look back.

Running past noisy cars and buildings of every shape and size, I finally reach the park, then stick to the shadows and slink along the fence until I reach a large pipe that runs under the ground, under the road outside the park, and empties into a dirty stream.

Here, I stop to lick my paws. My breathing slows, but my insides do not unwind. I do not understand how things went so wrong so fast. Was Tori upset that I left the apartment on my own? Did the strange man in the bakery, with his thin board and stack of papers, have something to do with how she squeezed me in the door? Or was Tori just the same as any other human with a bristly stick? Maybe I should not have trusted her or Lee or Pops or any other humans. Maybe humans are all the same.

Maybe every one of them, even Tori, has meanness inside them, like the dogcatcher and the boy with the stick. Maybe street life and the constant tug in my belly are better than the unexpected rip and shred of being turned on by someone I trust.

Lying against the cool metal side of the pipe, I rest and try to make myself small and invisible. When the sky outside the pipe darkens, I creep to the filthy stream, lap at the muddy water, then retreat to the pipe again. When the constant hum of tires on the road above slackens to just a buzz every now and then, I belly-crawl to the edge of the pipe. My paws ache to return to Tori, but I can't forget the angry look on her face when she brushed me with her stick and shoved the door closed on me.

My tongue sticks to the roof of my mouth. I need water—clean water, not the thick, sludgy mess pooling outside the pipe—so I venture out again. Darkness blankets the banks of the stream and the road above as I scramble upward.

When I peer over the edge of the ditch, the bright lights of an unexpected truck burn my eyes. I flick my head and flatten myself against the dirt wall until long after the rumble of the truck fades. Lifting my head again, I sniff for signs of strange dogs or stranger humans, but the patchy wind gusts from all the traffic make it difficult to tell the age of any scents.

Roadsides are full of danger. Big Guy taught me that long ago. But so is thirst, and right now, my dry tongue aches for clean water. So I drag myself from the ditch. I will return to the buildings closer to the alley, where I know I can find water. Stretching my neck, I glance one way then the other to check for traffic. All I see is a woman and boy standing in front of a lopsided car up the road a ways. The woman grips the boy's hand in one of hers. With the other, she holds a small talking box to her ear. I prick my ears, straining to make out her words.

"We . . . blowout . . . hurry . . . scared." Her head bobs back and forth on her neck as she examines the road. ". . . moving away . . . car . . . hits it."

Frightened chemicals gust from beneath her arms, the backs of her knees, inside her hands, everywhere, but I do not smell or see animals or anything else that should cause such fear.

"Uh-huh . . . just hurry." Her eyes dart one way, then the other. As she pulls the talking box away from her ear, it slips from her hand and clatters to the rocks on the side of the road. When she leans over to grab it, she drops the boy's hand. He bends to help, and their heads bang together.

"Ouch." His hand flies to the top of his head.

Just then, another enormous truck barrels up the road. Its bright lights flash on the boy's wide eyes. He blinks and stumbles into the road.

My body stiffens. I should look away, but I can't.

"Nooooo!" the woman screams, her face twisting into something scary, like anger but not exactly. When she yanks the boy away from the road, he squeals in pain, kind of like me when Tori swatted me with her bristly stick.

The truck blares. Tires screech. Smoke burns my nose. I step back, and my paws slip in the loose rocks and dirt at the side of the road. Clawing at the steep bank, I fight to stay near the road, where I can watch the humans. But it's no use. I slip down the dirt wall and land with a splat in the deep, muddy water below. The impact forces the air from my body. The weight of the thick, cold water presses down on me, pushing me deeper.

And deeper.

And deeper.

So deep, I can't take air in through my nose or mouth.

Chapter Twenty-Nine

The chilly stream where I land might not be good for drinking. It might be even worse for taking in air, but it's very good for numbing my burning paws and throat. It's also good for blurring the angry face of the woman on the side of the road. As I relax into the muddy cushion under the stream, the edges of the woman's face soften and melt like snow. In its softer form, her face no longer looks like that of a grown woman. Instead, it resembles the face of a young girl with waves of dark curls.

It's Tori, her face kind and full of light.

"In spite of everything, I still believe people are really good at heart," she reads the same calm words over and over. Then her jaw clenches. Her eyes bore into mine. "Watch me, Silly Millie. Get up," she commands like we're at dog class.

Forcing myself to look into her eyes, I dig deep inside for strength, then shove my paws into the mud. I slip, but soon, my head rises from the water.

"Good girl, Millie. Yes!" She beams. "You're such a good girl. You have such a big heart. Most dogs do. People too."

I cough and sputter. Water spews from my nose and mouth.

My head clears. But bits and pieces of the words she reads so often ring in my ears—especially the words, *people, good,* and *heart.*

People, good, heart.

People, good, heart.

With my head above water and air rushing into my nose and mouth, I realize I must pull myself from the muddy stream bed or risk leaving my body and this world behind forever. And I don't want to leave this world behind forever. I don't want to leave Little Pup before I've taught her all the things Bella taught me about wagging and head nuzzling and getting along in the human world. I don't want to leave Lee and Big Guy, who have families and packs of their own but who would still be very, very sad if they never saw me again. And I really, really do not want to leave Tori and Pops, who need a dog to rest their hands on and to give them a reason to get out of the apartment for something other than to go to school and to work at the bread place. So I twist and dig until I stand upright on all four paws.

I do not want to tangle myself up with the strange humans above me on the road, but I should check to make sure the emotional woman didn't hurt the small boy. So I drag my wet, tired body up the steep bank one more time.

A truck has joined the lopsided car on the side of the road. When I spot the woman and boy this time, they cling together, laughing and crying. A tall man walks toward them from the truck parked near their car.

"Are you okay?" The woman holds the boy away from her body, then presses her lips to his face over and over again.

"Mom, I'm fine." The boy laughs. "Stop."

She laughs, too, then squeezes him against her body again. "I thought that truck was going to hit you." She does not notice the approaching man. She has eyes only for the boy—much like Tori only ever has eyes for me when we're together or only ever had eyes for me until the bristly stick made her angry.

Sucking in the scent of the woman and boy, I smell the last bits of fear fading from their breath and skin but nothing like anger. The woman pulled the boy away from the speeding truck. She clearly cares about him, which is very confusing because she looked so angry before she pulled him to safety. Suddenly, I think of the busy family that took me in so long ago and how angry that mom looked when her boy screamed. What if she was more frightened for her son than she was actually angry at me? She was not a good dog person like Tori or Lee, but maybe she wasn't as mean as I believed either.

What if humans aren't that different from dogs? What if they show signs of anger when what they really feel is fear—kind of the way I used to bark and snarl and show my teeth when I wanted humans to give me space because I was scared?

What if Tori wasn't angry when she squeezed me in the door and swatted me with her bristly stick? What if she was scared? Maybe she needs me to save her from the man at the bakery with the thin board crooked in his arm.

Maybe tonight, instead of running and hiding or snapping and snarling when I feel frightened, I should try something different.

Chapter Thirty

As the black night sky fades to gray, I decide I will not run or hide. I will drag myself back toward Tori and Pops. Specks of light warm the silent buildings lining either side of the road. My nails drag the pavement on the trip back, which seems much longer than I remember. My side aches from the crashlanding in the stream and from being squeezed in the door, but I put one paw in front of the other and slowly make my way home.

That's what the apartment is now—my home. Tori and Pops are *home*. I thought the alley was my home, but the alley was just a place where I slept because I was too afraid to take another chance on humans. I thought I was safer on the streets, taking care of myself. But I was really just scared.

And if I've learned anything from Lee and Bella and Little Pup and Big Guy, it's that dogs are not meant to be alone. We're meant to have a pack, and usually, that pack is meant to be human. Bella and Lee are like two limbs growing from the same tree. Big Guy clearly believes he belongs with the woman in the flowy clothes and the floppy hat. Little Pup is bigger, stronger, and healthier with her humans than she ever was with me in the alley.

MILLIE

So I will be brave. I will return to the apartment. I will show Tori I will stay with her when she reads kindly from a book and also when she's angry or frightened by pointy, bristly sticks or by thin boards. I will stay with her forever.

So I lower my head and put one sore paw in front of the other.

But when I finally arrive at the apartment, the front door is shut tight. The room at the bottom of the stairs with the metal boxes on the wall is dark. Despite how badly I want to lie down and rest, I scratch at the door.

And scratch.

And scratch.

But no one comes to let me in.

So I half limp, half trot toward the end of this row of buildings and the alley. But just as I'm about to turn the corner, I hear the familiar *beep, beep, beep* of the trash truck and notice the trash cans dotting the sidewalk here and there.

My belly has been filled with human food for so long, and I was so intent on returning to the apartment, that I completely forgot about trash day. Now the noisy truck rolls onto the street in front of the bread place. When it stops a few doors up, the skinny man with the strange circles of glass over his eyes jumps down. He hoists a heavy can to the back of the truck. When it clunks back to the ground, he looks my way.

"Hey, Paul." He knocks on the side of the truck. "Look who's back—the little gremlin from last winter."

The man inside the truck lowers his glass and leans out. "How can you tell?" He tilts his head one way, then the other, like a dog sizing me up.

My pads moisten, but I do not run.

"See the beard?" The skinny man tosses a treat on the ground. "Here, little doggy."

Bella would go to the man. I might, too, I think, if I didn't need to find Tori so badly. Instead, I lift my tail and pump it back and forth, trying to show him I recognize him and appreciate the kindness and the treat, even if I don't have time to eat it right now.

"Look, she's wagging her tail. And I think she has a collar."

I lift my ears and the hair above my eyes to show him I'm friendly, then trot toward the alley to check the back door to the bread place for Pops and Tori. The sun will rise soon. Pops should not be far behind, so I curl up on the back step to wait.

And wait.

And wait.

I drift in and out of sleep.

But still, Pops does not arrive.

Chapter Thirty-One

When the sun finally peeks between the buildings and chases away the shadows in the alley, I know Pops and Tori are not coming. I must go, but I'm so thirsty my sides ache. Still, I drag myself to my paws and abandon the back stoop. As I pass the boarded-up entrance to my old nest, my insides squeeze. Even if I wanted to, which I certainly do not, I could not return to street life—not here in this alley anyway, not with the opening to the nest blocked. But I can't seem to return to apartment life right now either—not with Pops and Tori missing.

Little Pup cannot help me. She's still learning to take care of herself. I could not ask Big Guy to leave his woman even if I could find him. My tail droops. I don't want the dogcatcher to find me.

I know what Bella would do. She would find Lee. She would always find Lee. Lee is a good dog person and a good person person. Maybe, just maybe, if I could find Lee and Bella, they would help me find Pops and Tori, like they did once before.

So I do the only thing I know to do, I lower my nose to the ground and sniff for the road that leads away from the bakery and back toward the hole in the mountain far, far away. Now that the sun is rising in the sky, more and more humans trickle onto the streets. Today, they all seem to be moving toward the park, which is very strange. Normally, some humans move one way and some the other, but today, they all move straight toward the park. And today, they walk right down the middle of the street. There are no cars zipping back and forth. Sometime after the trash truck passed, while I was waiting on the back stoop, people raised boards that block the end of the road heading away from the bakery.

Hoping the snaking line of humans might lead me to my own people, I turn around and follow them away from the hole in the mountain and toward the park. One woman smiles. A child tugs at an adult's arm and points a chubby hand at me, but the humans seem so focused on reaching the park, they don't really notice me. Past the door to the apartment and past Little Pup's favorite place to squat, the tang of frying meat pulls at my nose. Loud music shakes the air.

"Welcome to the third annual Bark in the Park Spring Fling," a loud, sort-of-human, sort-of-mechanical voice interrupts the music blaring up the street.

I've heard those *Bark in the Park* words several times, but I don't have time to consider familiar words or any other words right now because a car with flashing lights sits near the entrance to the park. All the sharp smells, loud noises, and strange people overwhelm my senses. If I didn't want to find Tori so badly, I might actually want to curl up inside a kennel like the one with the soft blanket at the front of Lee's school room.

"Please check out the food trucks and vendors before the trick dog demonstration at twelve o'clock. And don't forget to visit the spring fling adoption festivities and raffles taking place

MILLIE

all day at the Humane Society booth." The tinny voice drones on and on.

The car at the park entrance with the flashing lights squawks. Then a woman in crisp, dark clothes and a stiff hat steps out. Her boots click the pavement menacingly. Dark circles cover her eyes. Her head turns. The dark circles scan the humans entering the park, then the road. Then they move to the sidewalk. When they land on me, I stumble.

The woman's mouth presses into a firm line.

The urge to squat pulls at my backside.

She unclips a talking box from her waist and pulls it to her mouth. "Homebase, this is Officer Downs, come in." Her dark circles remain locked on my face.

"This is base. Go ahead."

"We have a loose dog at the front gate. Could we get Animal Control or a Humane Society volunteer over here to help? Over." Her dark shiny shoes step toward me.

My heart pounds, threatening to rip from my chest.

"Sending someone now. Over."

The woman clips the talking box back to her waist, then rests her hand on the thick, short stick hanging from her pants.

I don't like her dark circles that resemble a wide-eyed dog ready to fight. I really don't like the way her strong hand grips the stick at her side. Lifting my nose to the air, I search for signs of Tori or Pops. I do not smell them, but under the heavy scent clouds of frying meat, I smell something sweet and wonderful. It's the sweet bread from the bread place, which can mean only one thing.

Pops.

And . . . Tori!

Despite the fear prickling every hair on my body, I step forward. I will not run. I will not hide. I will move past this woman in plain sight if it means finding Tori. So I raise a paw and take one step forward. And another. And another.

Then something horrible happens.

A heavy man with leather gloves exits the park gate and joins the woman in the dark, crisp clothes beside the car with the flashing lights. My nose twitches. He's too far away to identify by scent. But I don't need my nose to identify the long pole in his hands or the noose attached to it.

It's the dogcatcher.

I want to be brave. I want to charge past him through the gates and toward the scent of sweet bread inside the park. I want to find my girl. But if that man catches me, he'll take me straight to the shaking building with the frightened dogs and lock me in a cage, and I might not see Tori again. Ever.

And I cannot lose her now.

Not when I feel so close to finding her.

Chapter Thirty-Two

Head down, I scurry past a group of people approaching the gate, then duck behind a bench. The woman in the crisp, dark clothes and the dogcatcher block the entrance. I can't enter the park the way all the humans and their dogs on ropes are moving right now. I do not have a human to walk beside, and I do not have my rope.

But I do know a thing or two about outrunning humans. I may not be a street dog any longer, but I have not forgotten the ways of the street. I still know how to avoid capture, even if it's not because I want to be invisible.

"Watch out!" the dogcatcher shouts. His heavy feet pound the pavement behind me.

Ignoring him, I focus on Tori and the words she cares so much about—*people, good, heart*. I dart into the shadows of the trees lining the fence around the park, then slink toward the back road—the road where the angry-looking woman wrapped her arms so fiercely around her boy because she was so frightened.

The shadows shrink as I step into the hot light near the steep bank that falls away from the road and down to the murky stream. I do not want to *thwack* the mud beneath the thick water again, but I have to find Tori before the dogcatcher finds me.

I don't think she's in the apartment.

She's definitely not at the bakery.

I don't know what else to do, so I step onto the slippery pebbles at the edge of the steep bank and trust the tug of my nose toward the smell of the sweet bread inside the park. Slipping and sliding, I sit back on my behind to slow my descent. Dirt and rocks scrape and burn the sensitive skin under my tail. Today, I land with more of a gentle splash than a thundering *thwack*.

Staggering with thirst, I drag myself through the thick slop and scramble inside the cool pipe. Pausing to catch my breath, I enjoy the chill of the metal against my paw pads. A wave of wonderful smells crashes around me—fried meat, sweet bread, and many healthy dogs. Shaking my head, I clear muddy water from my ears and creep out the other end of the pipe. The music inside the park beats louder. Humans pack the park like the books on the shelf in Tori's room.

They wind this way and that in clumps. I do not recognize any familiar shapes or movements, but I do smell sweet bread and paper and maybe dried sticks. It's hard to tell if those smells belong to Tori, Lee, or Pops or if they are the leftover smells of the last time Tori, Lee, and I visited the park with Bella or if they just belong to similar-smelling humans.

As I lower my head for a better sniff, the music stops. The metal voice of a sort-of-human rings out. "The Humane Society raffles will start at two o'clock. You must be present to win. The winners of the first-ever Hearts and Hounds Writing Contest will be announced immediately after."

MILLIE

Digging deep inside for any last bit of strength, I force myself toward the swarm of people.

"Hey, there's a loose dog." A man reaches for me, but I'm too quick.

I scoot past him. A breeze ruffles the grass and stirs the smells that have settled there. My nostrils widen. My head lifts. My tail lifts. Despite my burning thirst, the corners of my mouth lift a little. My nose was right. The perfume of Pops's sweet bread blows into my face from the center of the park. So I stretch my neck, flatten my body, and gallop forward.

An older lady steps in my path and bends to reach for me. I hop sideways like a spring rabbit, racing full speed ahead toward a tiny building with wheels beneath it that gives off wave after wave of Pops's sweet-bread aroma. Ignoring the line of people standing out front, I leap up the stairs and through the door on the side of the tiny bread place on wheels.

But when I do, it's not Pops or Tori standing inside taking pieces of paper in exchange for bags of sweet bread; it's the hard-faced man from school—the hard-faced man who brushes the floor with his bristly stick—Mr. Crouse.

Desperate to reverse course, I plant my paws, but it's no use. I slide like Little Pup did through the snow last winter. My claws scrape the slippery floor.

Eyes wide, I slide directly toward the man's heavy, booted foot. My lips clamp tight against my teeth. My body stiffens in preparation for a horrible collision. When I hit Mr. Crouse's leg, it's like sliding headfirst into a brick wall in the alley. My head snaps backward as the rest of me slams to a sudden halt. Mr. Crouse doesn't grunt or shout. He glances down as if a pesky mosquito landed on his leg.

I do not know whether to bark and growl or duck and run, and it doesn't matter because my legs bend and collapse beneath me. My paws ache from days of scratching at doors and running on pavement. My dry tongue hangs from the side of my dry mouth. I remember Big Guy's lesson about the dangers of thirst.

But it's too late to worry about water, sore paws, or anything else because the inside of the strange bread place on wheels blurs. The gnarled hands of the massive man reach for me as I sink into the floor.

Deeper.

And deeper.

Until a foggy blanket of darkness swallows me whole.

Chapter Thirty-Three

When cold water dribbles down my tongue to my throat, I swallow gratefully.

"Good girl, Millie. Yes!" A familiar voice whispers. "She swallowed, Ms. Berry. I saw her."

"I saw it too." Another equally lovely voice answers.

It's Tori and Lee! Mustering all my strength, I open one eye as another trickle of deliciously clean water rinses the dryness from inside my lips. Tori lowers her face to mine and rubs her cheek against mine. I blink. My stiff body softens against the cool floor. I found her. I did it. I can relax.

"I'm so sorry, Millie." Tori's breath hitches in her throat when she speaks. "I'm so sorry. I didn't mean to hurt you. I was just so scared the inspectors would punish Pops if I let you in."

Despite my aches and pains, I thump my tail for her. A puppy-like yip shakes my jowls. My chest expands with more than air. Finding Little Pup was amazing. Finding Big Guy was glorious. Finding Tori is better than anything—better than finding a warm home on a cold day, even better than finding mountains of meat and eggs and cheese.

Lee smiles down at me from behind Tori. "She's going to be fine, Tori. We'll have Dr. Bassett, the volunteer vet, check her out just in case, but I think she's just hot, scared, and a little dehydrated. Mr. Crouse, can you angle that fan this way?"

"It's all my fault." Tori turns her wet eyes to Lee but does not forget to squeeze more drips of water from her bottle into my mouth.

Licking my lips, I give a stronger tail thump and try to show her I'm okay. We're okay. Everything will be okay now that we are back together. Plus, the large man, whose name must be Mr. Crouse, is not frowning, and he's not holding a bristly stick. He's holding something amazing. It's a spinning machine that blows cool air on my tummy and paws.

"Tori, you were trying to protect her and take care of your Pops. You could not have known she would run away. But she came back. She forgives you." Lee rests a strong hand on Tori's shoulder. "You need to forgive yourself."

"I just feel so bad." She pours a little more water on my tongue, then lowers her face to mine again.

When she does, I lick at the water sliding from the corners of her eyes. It's salty. I lick again and again.

"That tickles, Millie." Laughter bubbles from her lips like birdsong when she wipes her cheek.

"Now, that's more like it." Lee laughs too and softly claps her hands in front of her face.

I reach for Tori with my paw. She sits back on her behind, and I crawl into her perfectly sized lap and inhale the smell of sweet bread, young girl, health, and everything that makes her Tori. My head swivels at more familiar smells. Pops and Bella stand at the side door, peering in at us.

MILLIE

"You found her." Pops grips the side of the door and blinks his eyes. Bella leans against his leg like she's afraid he might fall over.

"This is very sweet." Mr. Crouse huffs, then bends down to hand Tori a small bowl of water with chunks of ice floating on top. "You know we're serving food here, right?" He nods at me.

"I know." Tori rubs dried dirt from my ears as I lap at the ice in the bowl. "And I don't care."

Water runs from the sides of my mouth. Except for my sore paws and empty belly, I feel almost as good as I did before I left the apartment to look for Tori. Now I understand why Big Guy always searched for water even before food. He must have had a falling-down experience like this, too, when he did not drink enough.

"You're the one who found her, Mr. Crouse, and got her help." Lee winks one eye at me and Tori. "I think you might be a dog person after all."

"I never said I didn't like dogs," he grumbles. "I just don't understand people taking them to schools or businesses. Or kitchens." He scowls at Lee. "They're perfectly fine for hunting or whatever."

"Good to know." Lee's top teeth press into her bottom lip, like she's biting back a smile. "So, you could actually be a dog person. I bet we could help you find a good one for hunting or . . . whatever."

He grunts. "If you don't mind, I've got customers to feed now that we've taken care of this emergency."

I can't be certain, but I think his face softens into something like a smile when he waves his arm to the opening at the front of the building.

"What does a grandfather have to do around here to be included?" Pops pulls himself up the stairs and inside the small bread place.

The strange building shifts under his weight as I wag for him.

His bones click when he lowers himself to the floor beside me and Tori and folds one leg over the other. He looks like a grown man trying to squeeze himself into the shape of a boy, but he smells wonderful, like sweet bread and dog kibble.

I nuzzle his pocket.

"I think she's going to be just fine too." Pops's eyes twinkle when he slips a plastic bag from his pocket. "It's my new signature dog treat, named just for you." He scratches me under the chin with his free hand.

I wag for him but can't take my eyes off the delicious-smelling bag in his hand.

"I call it the Millie Vanillie Liver Brownie." He breaks off a bit and offers it to me.

I swallow without chewing, then nudge his hand for more.

"Yeah, she's gonna be just fine." Lee shakes her head as Bella steps forward to sniff me from head to tail.

The crackling of the sort-of-mechanical, sort-of-human voice blaring through the park stops Bella midsniff. "Ladies and gentleman, if you haven't checked out the Humane Society raffles, there's still time. And . . . it's also time to announce the winner of the first ever Bark in the Park Young Writers Contest." The voice cuts off. The park hangs in silence. Then the voice resumes even louder this time. "This year's winner is Tori Smallwood for her poem 'All the Difference.'"

Tori's hand flies to her mouth.

"You entered?" Pops bumps his shoulder against Tori's.

"I did." Nervous smells suddenly gush from Tori's hands and behind her knees.

Pops zips the treat bag closed. I wag my tail, trying to remind Tori about the wonderful time we're having, but she doesn't seem to notice.

"Again, the winner is Tori Smallwood. Tori, please report to the Humane Society booth to collect your prize and to share your work. Ladies, gentlemen, dog lovers of every shape and size, if you're near the entrance to the nature trail at the back of the park, swing by the Humane Society booth to check out those raffles and to hear the winning entry read aloud in ten minutes."

Tori's mouth opens, but no words come out. Her hand stiffens on my head. She's not laughing. She looks like she might start panting.

Pawing her leg, I try to remind her that I'm right here, that we have cold water with chunks of ice to drink from Mr. Crouse, who doesn't seem so horrible after all. We have Pops's spectacular treats, and we have each other. We are together. We should be bouncing, wagging, and nuzzling.

Not freezing.

Stiffening.

Or panting.

Chapter Thirty-Four

Outside the small sweet-bread building on wheels, Tori stands with me and Bella and Lee and Pops near a raised wooden platform. I rest my behind on her foot to make sure she knows I'm not running away again. Ever. I will never, ever leave her—not even if she looks angry or holds a bristly stick. I've learned that sometimes humans hide their fear beneath snarling and snapping, just like dogs.

They can also hold more than one emotion at the same time, just like dogs. Bella can be a smiling, wagging yellow dog and also a firm top dog that will not let me chew baskets or dig in the couch all in the time it takes me to twitch my nose. Mr. Crouse can sound gruff and swish kids with a bristly stick, but he can also smile and give water with chunks of ice. I can be scared and want to run away at the same time that I also force myself to find Tori in a park crowded with strangers.

I will try to remember *people, good, heart* and not run away, even when I feel scared or when I'm surrounded by strangers, like the ones gathering around me and staring up at the empty platform. Suddenly, my nose wiggles at the familiar mixture of strong soap, the old girl dog from the kennel, and many other

MILLIE

dogs. It's Jada, and she's waving at us as she squeezes in between two clumps of people.

"Tori, congratulations. I'm so excited for you." She pats Tori on the back. Long twists of dark hair shimmer when her head bobs excitedly. "You won $250, and you get to share your poem with all these people."

Tori's mouth opens like it did earlier. Her head shakes, but she still doesn't make any words. She smells worried, almost sick, and I do not like it one bit. And I do not like the way she looks down at the ground but doesn't seem to see me right here, sitting on her foot.

Pops places a finger beneath her chin and lifts her face to his. They stare eye to eye. "Remember how we talked about leaning into things that scare us?"

She blinks.

"Remember how we talked about people changing—about Millie changing?" He leans closer to her face.

She breathes in slowly through her nose, closes her eyes, and nods.

"I would not let you go up on that stage if I didn't know you could do this. You're a writer, Tori. You've grown and changed this year. Now, go up there and be recognized." His fingers squeeze her shoulders.

Tori opens her eyes and looks to Lee.

"You're a reader, too, Tori. You read grade-level nonfiction. You can definitely read a poem you wrote yourself." Lee gently removes my rope from Tori's hand. "You can. Now, go."

Finally, Tori's eyes return to mine. My ears press tight against my face, but I wag, trying to show her that I'm scared, too, but I'm not running away. Then Jada takes Tori's hand and pulls her away from me.

I whine and tug at the rope clasped in Lee's hand, but she's too strong.

Tori is getting away from me, except she's not getting away exactly. She's climbing the steps to the wooden platform in front of us and following Jada to a skinny post.

"Ladies and gentlemen, dog lovers of all ages, please give a round of applause for Tori Smallwood, the winner of our first-ever Bark in the Park Young Writers Contest and her poem, 'All the Difference.'" Jada's voice rings out sort of like the blaring mechanical voice a little bit ago.

Tori's hands shake when she accepts the piece of paper Jada holds out to her. Jada motions to the skinny stick. Tori's eyes blink over and over when she steps forward. The small clumps of strangers around us go silent.

Tori lifts the flapping paper closer to her face. Her mouth opens again, but she still can't make words. I whimper. Something is horribly wrong. Humans use words from the time they are very small and never seem to run out of them. Why can't Tori make words now?

Pops and Lee nod and smile and shake their thumbs at the sky.

Tori swallows. Her mouth closes and opens. "Hi . . . I'm . . . uh . . . Tori. I . . . uh . . . wrote this"—she swallows again, like she has food stuck in her throat—"poem at school. After we read apoembyRobertFrost. It'scalled'AndThatHasMadeAll theDifference.'"

All of a sudden, words tumble from her mouth, sliding one into another without any pauses to take air into her body. Jada

MILLIE

steps forward and places a hand on her back. None of the strangers seem to take in air either. They know something is wrong too.

Tori glances at me. I lift my ears, trying to show her I'm listening. She nods, steadies the paper with her other hand, and shifts her eyes to Pops, like she's trying to tell him something with just her eyes.

"It's called 'All the Difference,'" she says. "Here goes:

> *I wanted a sister*
> *a sleep buddy*
> *a roommate*
> *a partner*
> *to listen*
> *to share*
> *to whisper*
> *from the other twin bed*
> *in the dark of night.*
>
> *I wanted a brother*
> *a teammate*
> *to stand strong*
> *to have my back*
> *claws out*
> *prepared to fight*
> *side by side.*
>
> *I wanted a family of my own*
> *to keep me safe*
> *and guard my heart.*
>
> *I wanted a home*
> *a castle*
> *a fortress*

*stone walls
to wrap me
inside a hedge of protection.*

*I wanted a best friend
a prankster
a partner in crime
with a gentle tongue
and good ears.*

*I got all that
and more
when I found a dog.*

*I won the trophy
the blue ribbon
the lottery, the grand prize.*

*I found Millie
And that has made all the difference.*

    She stares at Pops, like one top dog appraising another. He wipes dirt or something from his eyes but does not look away. A couple people sniff like their noses are wet. Then Lee lifts her hands to clap, and I charge like a mother defending her pups. Lee's hand tightens on the rope but not fast enough. I dart between the legs of a woman near the platform and fling myself up the steps toward Tori.

    Collectively, groups of humans suck in air when they realize I'm free. A dog barks like he thinks I'm inviting him to play chase. The rope smacks the ground behind me. Tori's head whips in my direction.

    We lock eyes, and I hurl myself into her outstretched arms.

The crowd explodes. Tori's paper flutters to the ground when she buries her face in my wiry coat.

Jada steps to the skinny post. "Well, if that's not a testament to the special bond between a human and her dog, I don't know what is." She wipes at her eyes too. "And if your home and your heart have room for something like that, we still have a really sweet old girl in need of a forever home up for adoption. Come see me if you're interested, but first, how 'bout one last round of applause for Tori Smallwood."

The humans clap and clap and clap, even after Tori accepts some papers from Jada, carries me off the platform, and sets me on the ground. Smiling people pat Tori on the back as we pass, and they say things like *beautiful* and *good job*.

Pops pulls Tori into his arms as we approach. Bella and I bounce around their feet when Lee pulls both of them into her arms.

"Pops?" Tori squirms free. "We have to keep her. Please?" Her eyes beg like a puppy's.

Pops's face cracks.

"The adoption stuff is winding down for the day too." Lee reaches down and ruffles my ears. "In fact, Bella and I need to go check on Jada to see if she's having any luck finding a home for the old girl from class."

Tori rocks forward on the front of her feet. "Does that mean—"

Lee shakes her head. "That means you talk to your Pops. I suggest you do it over ice cream and celebrate the first of what I'm sure will be many writing awards." Lee pats her leg and Bella follows.

MILLIE

Shoulders sagging, Pops watches them go, then shakes his head, and works his mouth back into a smile. "Lee's right. Millie goes home with us today. We'll talk about long-term plans after we get some rest and celebrate your big win. But first, something for Millie." He pulls the bag of treats from his pocket and breaks off another bite of deliciousness for me, then offers his crooked arm to Tori. "And ice cream for you."

Tori slips her skinny arm through the bend in his. "Come on, Millie. We're gonna eat ice cream."

I wag my tail and follow. Whatever we are about to eat must be fabulous, because Pops is smiling, really smiling, in his eyes and everything, for the first time since I can't remember when.

Chapter Thirty-Five

Back at the apartment, long after Tori falls asleep curled around my body, I hear bits and pieces of the words Pops whispers into his talking box in the kitchen.

"Yes . . . dog . . . could . . . some stability . . ."

He takes long pauses, which I think means a voice is talking back to him from inside the box, even if I can't hear it.

"I guess . . . true . . . that poem . . ." His words drag long and slow until they almost fade away completely. "Yes . . . agree . . . good night."

Holding my eyes open in the dark, I wait and wait and wait until his feet finally scuff down the hall to his room. When his bed squeaks under his body, I close my eyes and don't open them again until the sun shines into the room and lights Tori's face. When I begin to pant from the heat of the covers and Tori's body and the rays of sun streaming through the window, I carefully pull myself to a cooler spot on the bed and wait for Tori's eyes to open.

But her hand reaches for me before she opens her eyes, like she knows even in sleep when our bodies are separated. Resting my head on her outstretched hand, I show her that I am still here. When her eyes finally open, they look directly into mine, and she smiles.

"Hey, Silly Millie! I'm so glad you're here." She touches the side of my face.

I lick her hand.

Then she's up, pulling on shoes, and taking me outside to my favorite tree to do my business. Today is not a Tori-and-Millie day, but that is okay because I am still very tired from my time on the street and need to sleep on the couch for a while until Pops and Tori return to the apartment. I need to rest up for dog class and for Little Pup, so I nestle down in the couch, close my eyes, and breathe in the smell of Tori until Ms. Smith comes to take me potty.

Once I come back inside, I nestle some more until I finally hop down from the couch and lie beside the door to wait.

My tail wags my body when Tori's scent squeezes through the crack under the door.

"Hey, Silly Millie!" she says as the door swings open. Then she lifts me to her chest, squishes her lips to my face over and over, and loops a rope around my head. "Let's go potty," she says as she places me back on the floor.

After potty and dinner, we walk to dog class instead of riding in the car. A soft breeze ruffles the wiry hairs of my outer coat. Tori gives me lots of slack on the rope to sniff. While she and Pops talk and talk, I sniff and sniff.

"Your mom and I made a decision." Pops's voice drops. He sounds very serious all of a sudden, but I do not worry because we're headed to dog class. Tori's pockets are loaded with treats, and we will get to see Little Pup very soon.

But then Tori suddenly stops. The rope attached to my neck tightens. I turn and sniff to see if something, like a squirrel or a strange dog, has caught her attention. An older woman and man walk hand-in-hand down the other side of the street—nothing too exciting about that.

"An-d?" Tori's word breaks in the middle, making her sound young and small.

"And . . ." Pops repeats the same word, dragging it out long and slow.

My head swivels back and forth between the two of them, even though I really just want to keep sniffing the sidewalk.

"And she and I agree that Millie is good for you—for all of us, really." He smiles down at me. "We don't know exactly what the future is going to look like, but we know it looks better with Millie in it. And we're committed to making that happen, even if it gets a little complicated."

Tori flings her arms around Pops almost as fiercely as the woman with the boy on the side of the road did several nights ago. Tori's not angry, though, because her smile stretches almost from one ear to the other. When she turns toward me, she bends and claps her hands. I leap into her arms the way I did the day everyone clapped for her on the raised platform at the park.

Pops wraps us in his arms, then presses his lips to the top of Tori's head and then mine.

"And one other thing?" His forehead creases when his eyebrows rise on his face.

Tori lifts her chin from my head to look at him.

"The social worker at the treatment center gave your mom permission to start weekly visits this week. Your mom wants

MILLIE

me to text her and let her know if it's okay if she comes to watch dog class tonight."

Tori hugs me tighter to her chest like she's frightened, but there's nothing to be frightened of here—certainly not the older man and woman on the other side of the street.

"You do not have to say *yes*, Tori. She's more than willing to visit another time, another place, whatever is comfortable for you."

"No." Tori shakes her head. "I mean yes. Yes, I'd like her to see Millie take the test tonight. She can come."

When Tori says my name, I soften my body and sink into her chest, the way Bella smiles and leans into Lee's leg when she says Bella's name.

"Silly Millie." Tori rubs her face against mine. "I think that means we better ace this test—even the greeting-the-friendly-stranger part."

I don't understand all her words, but I like the way it sounds when she calls me *Silly Millie*.

Chapter Thirty-Six

When we enter the building for dog class, I wag for Lee and Bella. I also wag for Little Pup and her humans when Tori leads me past them to my little table at the end of the line of dogs and their humans. Little Pup wags and smiles too. Her paws tip-tap the top of the table where she stands, but she does not jump down or flop on her back to wiggle. My chest expands. She is learning.

The scent of strange humans pulls my face away from her. The old girl dog from the shelter stands with a person who smells like cleaning supplies and many children. Wait. He is not a new person. He's just new to dog class. It's Mr. Crouse, and he seems to have left his bristly stick at school.

"Welcome, everyone," Lee speaks in her top-dog voice. "I want everyone to take a deep breath. There's nothing to be nervous about. We will conduct the Canine Good Citizen test like any other class. I'll have you and your dogs run through one skill at a time, but tonight, I'll check you off on my clipboard. If you or your dog make a minor mistake, you'll have one chance to try again. If anyone is excused for any reason, like inappropriate fear or shyness, you'll have an opportunity to repeat the

MILLIE

class and take the test again in six to eight weeks. So, there's nothing to worry about."

I rock back on my behind to rest. When Lee starts talking at dog class, sometimes it seems like she will never finish.

"We might also have a couple visitors this evening—" The bells on the door jingle, interrupting her words.

It's David, strolling in with his hands shoved into his pockets and smelling a little uncertain. His body relaxes when Lee waves at him, and he lifts his hand to return the gesture.

Lee turns back to the group. "This is my . . . friend David. He and I have a date after class. And I brought another friend tonight. In case you didn't see Zeus on the way in, he's the Rottweiler mix in the crate beside Tori's grandfather and Jada. He was rescued from a horrible situation, so I'm taking it really slow with him."

Jada waves at the group. "Don't forget to introduce Mr. Crouse."

I'm happy to see David and Jada and all the people I've met since my time on the street, but I grow very bored by all of Lee's long strings of words. I would really like to get to the part where Tori gives me many treats.

"Oh." Lee's hand flies to her chest. "How could I forget? Everyone, this is Jim Crouse. He's a custodian at my school. He adopted—"

"I'm calling her Edith." Mr. Crouse leans down to run his knotty hand along the old girl dog's side. "I figured she couldn't cause much trouble, and us old folks have to stick together."

The long rope of hair hanging down Lee's back almost seems to wag when she laughs.

"Awwww. How wonderful." The lady with the stick-legged dog makes happy baby sounds when she pats her hands together and smiles at Mr. Crouse.

His shoulders rise and fall when he smiles at the old girl.

Tori sits on the table beside me and lowers her mouth to my ear. "Just like Anne Frank, Millie." She ruffles the hair around my neck and exhales like she's also tired of all this talking.

Then the bells on the door jingle again. Now a woman with waves of dark curls steps hesitantly into the building. The humans all turn to watch. The dogs inhale the scent of her. Air catches in Tori's throat. My eyes flash from her to Lee to Pops, searching for any sign of danger. Pops's knuckles whiten on the arms of his chair as he pushes himself up to greet the new woman.

"Hi, Dad," the woman, who somehow reminds me of Tori, whispers.

"Hi, Vanessa." Now air catches in his throat when he talks.

The woman lifts her hand toward Tori, then lets it fall back to her side. A hint of something both excited and nervous leaks from inside Tori's hands.

"This is Tori's mom, Vanessa," Pops says to the group.

The humans mumble greetings. Tori lifts a hand.

"Welcome." Lee claps her hands together. "We're so glad you're here. If you like dogs, you can be the friendly stranger for a couple of the exercises. I was going to use David, but that's not really fair because Millie's met him before."

The woman, who looks like Tori, wipes her hand on her short pants. "Sure. Just tell me what to do."

"Great. We'll go ahead and get started, then." Words and more words tumble from Lee's mouth the way they always do at dog class.

I look up at Tori's eyes, but for once, they're not looking back at me. They're still watching the woman with the dark waves of hair so much like her own.

"You'll start down here," Lee says and points to the huffing man and the huffing dog with the flat face at the other end of the line of tables. "You'll walk up to the person, say something, like, 'Good evening, cute dog,' or whatever, then shake hands with the dog's handler, then say, 'Have a good day,' and move to the next dog and handler."

"Seems easy enough," the woman says as she steps toward the huffing man and dog.

"Okay, everyone, seat your dogs at your side on the ground. Remember, no treats during the exam. You can begin," Lee says to the woman with the waves of dark hair, then scratches a piece of paper with a thin stick of wood as the woman moves from one person to the next.

As she gets closer, the nervous, excited smells leaking from Tori spike. The woman gives off almost exactly the same smells. It's almost like the woman belongs to Tori or the other way around.

As the woman approaches Little Pup and her humans, Little Pup begins to squirm. Her backside wiggles. "Easy, Skittles," the boy holding her rope says.

When she settles, my insides grow and expand. The little ball of fluff from the alley has been replaced by a good dog that will do just fine in the human world.

The new woman seems nice enough, even though Tori smells very worried and excited about her. I wonder if there's something I'm missing. Flicking my nose to Pops, I inhale the scent of him. He smells concerned, too, and his foot taps the floor nervously. Bella's tail thumps the raised bed where she rests in the center of the room. Lee's body flows smooth and calm, like a river, like the first time I met her.

My pads moisten as the dark-haired woman steps in front of me. A whimper rises in my throat. I don't like the conflicting signals coming from Tori and Lee and Pops and Bella. I have no choice but to trust my own instincts, and my instincts tell me that even though Tori and Pops are worried, this woman does not pose a threat to us at the moment.

So I sit very still and watch as Tori and the woman greet each other. When they squeeze hands, energy passes between them, and they smile.

"I like your dog." The woman searches Tori's eyes when she speaks, like she lost something inside of them.

My tail sweeps the floor.

"This is Millie. She's pretty amazing." Tori smiles down at me, then meets and holds the woman's eyes. Their hands remain clasped, like they've forgotten the greeting is usually just a squeeze and release.

"Excellent. Excellent." Lee scratches her paper again.

The worried smells loosen and fade as the woman walks back to Pops and takes a seat, which is wonderful. But I grow very bored with this class. Not only does Lee talk even more than usual, but Tori also does not give me any treats, even when I sit quietly and stare into her eyes for a very long time, even when I do *sit* and *down* as soon as she asks.

After each dog does *come* from the end of a very long rope, Lee places her thin board on the floor beside Bella's bed. "Huge congratulations! You all passed. I'll send your paperwork in to the American Kennel Club tomorrow, and you'll receive your certificates in the mail in a few—"

Jada claps her hands together, interrupting Lee's very long string of words. Pops, David, and the dark-haired woman join in. Bella sits up and wags. Little Pup's boy bends down to scratch the good spot near her tail.

I wag and wag and wag, trying to show Tori that I would like a good scratch near the tail spot as well. Thankfully, she lifts me to her chest, which is even better, and carries me toward the dark-haired woman.

"Great job, ladies." Pops holds his hand up for Tori to slap.

When Tori's hand falls, she turns to the woman with the matching hair. "Hi, Mom."

"Tori . . ." The woman brushes a loose curl away from her face with a shaky hand. "You look great. You've grown so much and trained a dog and . . . won a writing contest—all in a few months."

"You look good too." When Tori lifts her chin, she's almost as tall as the woman. "What do you think about Millie?"

"She's even more adorable than I expected. Can I pet her?"

Tori nods. The woman's hand brushes Tori's when she pets my back, and they look deep into each other's eyes again. When they lean into me and lean into each other, their breathing slows. The fear scents fade and shift into something calmer. They don't look away until Little Pup bounces past with her humans. She barely even tugs on her rope as she leads the large man and his boy to the door. Bells jingle as they leave, followed by other dogs and humans.

"We're gonna head out," Pops calls across the room to where Lee and Bella stand talking to David and Jada.

As Tori places me on the floor, David reaches for Lee's hand and winds his fingers through hers. All the clapping and petting and holding of human hands tonight is nice. It almost makes up for all Lee's talking and the lack of treats. Almost but not quite.

"I'll see you after school tomorrow, Mack. Nice to meet you, Vanessa." Lee waves her free hand at us.

"Want to walk with us?" Pops asks the woman whose name must be Vanessa.

"I'd love that, Dad." She turns very slowly toward Tori, like she doesn't want to scare her away. "Is that okay?" she asks.

"Yes, I can show you some of Millie's tricks."

Pops pushes the door open for us. I wag at the sound of my name as the bells jingle behind us. Streetlights hum overhead as we turn onto the street that leads back to the apartment. My head jerks at the tinkle of laughter from the other side of the street. A very well-fed dog leads a laughing girl along the street. They're followed by a woman who fits perfectly under the arm of the man in the hat beside her. Even from this distance, I recognize them. It's the family from the other end of town. They live in the house that smells like mountains of meat.

The last time I saw them, I did not know my name. I was a street dog hiding behind a trash can, shivering in the dark of night and afraid of my own shadow. Now, I am Millie. When they approach, I do not tuck tail and run. I stand tall in a pool of light on a warm summer night and wag for them.

"Good girl, Millie. Yes!" Tori looks right at me and feeds me many bits of cheese when I do not shy away from the unfamiliar man in the hat.

I swallow without chewing, tilt my head back, and howl with joy. I feel full inside, and it's not from the tiny bits of yummy cheese Tori feeds me.

It's a fullness that comes from *people, good, heart*.

From learning my name, finding my dogs, and finding my people.

From seeing the best in others and allowing them to see me—to know me—the real me, outside of the shadows.

From standing tall and unafraid in a circle of bright light with my pack.

With my family.

With my very own girl.

Discussion Questions

1. At the beginning of the book, Millie overhears the family on the street discussing preparations for the upcoming snowstorm. The dad of the family says all he needs is food, family, and shelter to survive. Do you agree or disagree that these are a human's most important needs? What would you add to or take off the list? Explain.
2. Millie learns new skills in order to adapt to life on the street, at the shelter, and in an apartment with her new family. Think about a time you struggled to learn something new but eventually acquired the skill or mastered the content. What challenges did you face? How did you overcome the challenges? What kind of help did you receive from others? What did you learn about yourself from these struggles?
3. People who do not know Millie well often mistake her fear for aggression. Think about a time when a teacher, parent, or friend misunderstood your behavior. How did that feel? How did you handle the misunderstanding?
4. Jada tried to discourage Lee from rescuing Millie, but Lee trusted her own intuition and Bella's. Would you have trusted your instincts? Did Lee make a wise choice based on what she did or did not know about Millie? Explain.

5. Millie develops close relationships with Tori and Lee. Which human do you think helps Millie grow and learn the most? Explain.
6. Important characters in stories usually change throughout the story. How does Millie change from the beginning of the story to the end?
7. Books and stories include lessons, morals, and themes the characters learn and internalize. Millie learns several important lessons over the course of the story. Which lesson or theme do you think is the most important? Explain.
8. Pick one of your favorite scenes in the book that does not include an illustration. Using specific details and examples from the story, explain the scene to a partner or draw a picture of the scene to share with the class.
9. When Tori's class reads *The Miraculous Journey of Edward Tulane*, they discuss what it means "to be known." What do you think it means "to be known"? How does true belonging feel? Explain.
10. Anne Frank was a Jewish girl who kept a diary about her experiences in hiding during the Holocaust. She witnessed firsthand horrible acts committed by some humans against others. In spite of that, she still believed "people [were] basically good at heart." Do you agree? Why or why not?

Dog Training Tips

Getting Started

Gather what dog trainers, such as Lee, call high-value treats—yummy treats that easily break into tiny bits without making crumbs. Small bits of string cheese work well, but all dogs have different tastes. Try various treats until you know what really excites and motivates your dog.

All dogs, but especially picky or less food-motivated ones, will be more eager to work and learn in exchange for treats before a meal than when their bellies are full.

Remember to adjust the size of your dog's meals based on how many treats it gets during a training session. If you are very generous with bits of bacon or store-bought treats, be sure to decrease the amount of food you feed your dog at its next meal.

Find a quiet, familiar place to train, away from distractions, such as other pets, siblings, or very interesting smells.

Timing is everything in dog training. You want your verbal praise and food treat to be as immediate as possible so that you "capture" the behavior you want, as Lee explains to Tori outside the bakery. The better you time the praise, such as, "Yes," or, "Good girl," and the delivery of the treat, the faster your dog will understand what you're asking it to do.

Training Exercises

Some dog trainers start with *watch me*. Some start with *sit*. We're going to start with *sit*.

Have a few treats in your hand, ready to go. Have additional treats on a nearby counter or in a fanny-pack-type pouch around your waist, where you can get to them quickly and easily without wasting time.

SIT

- Stand in front of your dog. If you've chosen a yummy, tasty-smelling treat, your dog will naturally lift its eyes and head to watch. This movement will shift your dog's weight toward its rear end. Let that shift in weight help you as a trainer. In one smooth, slow motion, lower your treat toward your dog's forehead, then back over the top of its head toward its shoulders. If your timing is perfect, which is not very likely on your first try, or you are very lucky, your dog will rock backward to follow the treat with its eyes and naturally, or accidentally, depending on how you look at it, sit.

- If your dog sits on purpose or on accident, immediately use brief, clear verbal praise—something like, "*Yes*," or, "*Nice*"—and deliver the treat in time with the word as best you can. If you can time the delivery of the treat with the exact moment your dog's rear end hits the floor, your dog is going to learn more quickly.

- Most of us are not that lucky. Usually, we move our hand a little too quickly or a little too slowly, as Lee explains to Tori. If we move our hand too slowly, our dog may lean forward to reach for the food, which we do not want. If we move our hand too quickly, our dog may twist to look for the treat over its shoulder.

- Watch your dog's eyes, and move slowly enough that it can track the treat with its eyes but not so slowly that it's tempted to reach or lunge for the food.
- Do not give your dog the treat if it doesn't sit. If you do, you might capture a behavior that you do not want, and your dog will try to repeat the behavior you don't want instead of the *sit* that you do want.
- Be patient. If your dog is struggling, try moving your hand a little faster or a little slower. You can also try moving the treat a little closer or farther from your dog's face. If you need additional help, go online with an adult and visit a reliable website, such as The American Kennel Club's, and watch videos on teaching puppy manners or basic obedience skills.

WATCH ME

Dogs do not normally look directly into each other's eyes without a reason. So be patient with your dog when teaching *watch me*.

- Stand in front of your seated or standing dog. Hold your tiny, yummy-smelling treat in front of or at the corner of your eye. The second your dog looks at the treat and your eye, say, "*Yes*," and quickly deliver the treat. Do this several times. Deliver praise and your treat the second your dog looks into your eye.
- When you think your dog is starting to understand, begin using the *watch me* command with the treat held near your eye. Say, "*Watch me.*" The second your dog looks in

the direction of your eyes and the treat, say, "*Yes*," and give it the treat. Do this three to four times per day at different times and in different locations.

- When you think your dog is starting to understand the actual command *watch me*, try waiting one second before saying *yes* and delivering the treat. If your dog looks away before one second, it's confused about what's being asked of it and what it's being rewarded for. Go back and do several *watch me*'s and deliver the praise and treat without any wait time. When you think your dog is ready, try the treat and command with one second of wait time again. Be patient. As your dog gets better, extend the wait time to two seconds, then three.

- When your dog gets to several seconds, you can try different positions, such as having your dog seated beside you. You can also begin pinching the treat farther and farther back on your finger so that your dog sees less and less of the actual treat and is transitioning to looking at just your finger and not the treat.

- Eventually, you will be able to point at your eye with just your finger, say, "*Watch me*," then pull the treat from your pocket or waist pouch and deliver it. If at any time your dog fails to hold your gaze for the wait time you've been practicing two or three times in a row, that means you're moving too quickly, and your dog needs to take it a little slower. When this happens, and it happens to every dog and human at some point, simply reduce the amount of wait time, and give your dog the opportunity to feel successful before slowly increasing the time again.

Final Notes on Dog Training and Safety

- Only train your own dog—one you know and trust and that knows and trusts you.
- Always train with an adult nearby, should you need help for any reason.
- Most importantly, if you ever feel yourself getting frustrated with yourself or your dog, stop training. Dog training is all about two entirely different species learning to communicate and trust each other. This important relationship cannot be fostered if you are feeling frustrated or your dog is feeling anxious. When you or your dog become frustrated, which will happen at some point, especially if you go on to train at higher levels, stop training, go for a walk, or play something your dog enjoys, such as fetch. Try training again after a long break, or wait until the following day.
- To become a skilled dog trainer like Lee takes a lot of patience, a lot of practice, and a very long time. Be patient with yourself and your dog. Celebrate every success, no matter how tiny, and consider asking an adult if you and your dog can enroll in a beginner obedience class. Local kennel clubs will frequently offer discounts for junior handlers. Junior handlers are what groups such as The American Kennel Club call people eighteen years old and younger who compete in dog sports and activities.
- Go to the library and check out books on dog behavior and dog training. Research videos and other training resources online with an adult. Enroll in a class with your dog, and above all, have fun.